DREAMWORKS

Spirit

RIDING FREE

The
Adventure Begins

Little, Brown and Company
Hachette Book Group
1290 Avenue of the Americas, New York, NY 10104
Visit us at LBYR.com

Originally published in hardcover and ebook by Little, Brown and Company in May 2017
First Paperback Edition: May 2019

Little, Brown and Company is a division of Hachette Book Group, Inc. The Little, Brown name and logo are trademarks of Hachette Book Group, Inc.

The publisher is not responsible for websites (or their content) that are not owned by the publisher.

Library of Congress Control Number 2017932038

ISBNs: 978-0-316-42506-3 (pbk.), 978-0-316-55786-3 (ebook)

Printed in the United States of America

LSC-C

Printing 3, 2021

OFFICIAL
MARK OF
SPIRIT

RIDING FREE

The Adventure Begins

SUZANNE SELFORS

Little, Brown and Company

New York Boston

Introduction

A buckskin stallion stood at the edge of his herd, his head held high, his eyes alert. While the other horses filled their bellies with tender spring grass, his gaze swept the prairie. Leaves rustled in the breeze. Butterflies flitted among stalks of milkweed. A toad leaped onto a rock, to bask in the morning sun.

All appeared peaceful.

The stallion sniffed the air for hidden signs of danger. No damp scent of wolf. No musky scent of bear. And no people, with their strange odors of fire and soap. His ears pricked, listening for anything that might cause trouble, but he was greeted with a gentle trickle from a nearby creek and the lazy whistle of a meadowlark as it called to its mate. The stallion nodded with contentment.

He lowered his head and nibbled the sweet grass, his tail flicking once, twice, to chase away a dragonfly. But on this morning, grazing wasn't on his mind. He lifted his head again, his legs stiffening. The prairie stretched before him, a vast, wide-open space, and it was calling. He stomped his hoof and snorted. The others understood, for he was young and restless. They stepped aside. His sister gazed at him. *Go*, her eyes said.

Checking once more to make sure the herd was safe, he took a deep breath. Then he reared up and…

…charged!

Nothing stood in his way. No mountains, no rivers, no houses or train tracks. With his face in the wind, he was filled with immeasurable joy. He was free.

The morning sun warmed the prairie as the stallion's galloping hooves beat their wild rhythm.

Part One

1

The morning sun streamed through the windows as Lucky's shoes beat their wild rhythm.

Though Lucky was a natural runner, with long, strong legs, the shoes themselves hadn't been designed for such activity. Made from stiff black leather, with a half-inch heel, they laced tightly up the shins. That very morning the boots had been polished to a perfect sheen by the family butler. If she kept running, Lucky would surely develop blisters, but she didn't have far to go.

With no one around to witness, Lucky picked up speed and darted down the hallway of Madame Barrow's Finishing School for Young Ladies. Running within school walls was strictly prohibited, along with other disrespectful activities like pencil gnawing and gum chewing. But sometimes rules had to be broken, especially when a hot, buttered scone was at stake. So Lucky ran as fast as she could, her long brown braid thumping against her back. Morning tea at Barrow's was a tradition the headmistress had brought with her from England. The school's cook could make the pastry so flaky it practically melted in the mouth. And she stuffed each one with a huge dollop of salted butter and sweet blackberry jam. Lucky's mouth watered just thinking about it. But she was late. So very late. Which wasn't entirely her fault.

There'd been a…*distraction.*

She'd been looking out the window as she tended to do during morning recitations, her mouth moving automatically, for she knew her multiplication tables by heart. "Twelve times five is sixty. Twelve times six is seventy-two." Her legs felt twitchy, as they often did when she was forced to sit for long periods of time. "Twelve times seven is eighty-four. Twelve times eight is ninety-six."

"Lucky, please stop fiddling," the teacher said.

"Yes, ma'am." Lucky sat up straight and tucked her feet behind the chair legs to keep them still.

"Continue, everyone."

"Twelve times nine is—"

Lucky stopped reciting. Something on the other side of the street caught her eye. It was a horse, but not the usual sort that one saw in the city. This horse wasn't attached to a carriage or wagon. A bright-red blanket lay across his back and feathers hung from his black mane. He was being led down the sidewalk by a man whose long blond hair was topped by a cowboy hat. The fringe on the man's pants jiggled as he walked. Certainly the city was full of colorful people who came from every corner of the world, but Lucky had never seen a cowboy in person, only in photographs. He walked in a funny, bowlegged way and was handing out pieces of paper to passersby. Lucky leaned closer to the window, but a carriage pulled up and blocked her view.

"Twelve times fourteen is..." Lucky tapped her fingers on the desk. She couldn't get that cowboy and his beautiful horse out of her mind. What were they doing in the city?

"Lucky. Please sit still!"

And so it was that after recitations, instead of heading to tea with the other students, Lucky snuck out the front door to see if the cowboy was still there.

He wasn't. And by that time, morning tea had already begun.

The headmistress believed that teatime was as crucial to a young lady's education as literature or history because it taught manners and the important art of conversation. Plus, she insisted that the tea they served at Barrow's Finishing School was superior because it came all the way from England and had a picture of Queen Victoria on the tin. Lucky wasn't a huge fan of the stuff, but those scones were to die for.

She bounded up the flight of stairs, lifting her long skirt so she wouldn't get tangled. She detested the school uniform—a stiff white blouse that buttoned all the way to the chin and a gray wool skirt that always seemed too heavy and too hot. She'd pleaded many times for a change in uniform. She'd brought in newspaper articles to show the headmistress that pants were all the rage in other countries. But her reasonable request fell on deaf ears, for the headmistress was as immobile as a ship in the sand. "My young ladies will not be seen in public in a pair of bloomers!"

Lucky leaped onto the second-floor landing. From the end of the hall came the clinking of china and the quiet conversations of her fellow students. She was almost there. Still gripping her skirt, she dashed out of the stairwell, turned sharply on her heels, and then raced down the hall.

Only to bump into something.

Correction—into *someone*.

When a scone-craving, restless student collides with a no-nonsense, uppity headmistress, the impact is the stuff of legend. Not only was the wind knocked out of both parties, but they were thrown off-balance. Objects flew into the air—a notebook, a hair comb, a marble pen. When Lucky reached out to break her fall, she grabbed the first thing in front of her, which happened to be the headmistress's arm. Down they both tumbled, landing on the hallway carpet in a most unladylike way. Lucky knew this was bad—very bad. The headmistress had probably never sat on the ground in her entire life, let alone been knocked down to it!

Madame Barrow pushed a stray lock of hair from her eyes. "Fortuna. Esperanza. Navarro. Prescott!" she said between clenched teeth.

"Gosh, I'm so sorry," Lucky said, scrambling to her feet. "I didn't see you." She offered a hand to the headmistress, pulling her up off the carpet. Then she collected the hair comb, notebook, and pen. "Are you hurt?"

Madame Barrow, headmistress of Barrow's Finishing School for Young Ladies, did not answer the question. Instead, with expertly manicured fingers, she brushed carpet fuzz off her perfectly pressed gray skirt. She set her hair comb back into place, collected the pen and notebook, and then drew a focused breath, filling her lungs as if she were about to dive underwater. Lucky could have sworn that the intake of oxygen added another inch to the headmistress's towering frame. Silence followed. Agonizing silence. Then, after a long exhale, the headmistress spoke. "Do you know how long I have been teaching young ladies of society?" she asked in her thick British accent.

"No, Madame Barrow." Lucky tried not to stare at the headmistress's right eyelid, which had begun to quiver with rage.

"Fifteen years, Miss Prescott. Fifteen *dedicated* years." With a flourish of her hand, she began what Lucky expected would be a long, *dedicated* lecture. "I was raised and educated in England, Miss Prescott, a country that is the pillar of civility and tradition. The patrons of this institution have placed the tender education of their daughters in my capable hands. In my fifteen years here, I have encountered many different sorts of young ladies. But never, and I repeat, *never*, has one child exhibited so much... *spirited energy*."

Spirited energy? Lucky fidgeted. "I know I'm not supposed to run, but—"

The headmistress held up a hand, stopping Lucky mid-excuse. A moment of uncomfortable silence followed. At the other end of the hall, a few students poked their heads out of the tearoom. Eavesdropping. Who could blame them? The scene in the hall was oodles more interesting than the idle chitchat they were forced to engage in while sipping tea. "Must I remind you that running *inside* is not appropriate behavior for a young lady of society?"

"Yes, Madame Barrow. I mean, no, you don't need to

remind me." Lucky shuffled in place. Sarah Nickerson's head appeared next to the others. She smirked. Lucky wanted to holler, "Mind your own business, Sarah!" But she didn't.

"And yet…you ran." The headmistress raised an eyebrow. Lucky scratched behind her ear. She was starting to feel itchy, as if allergic to the headmistress's intense and unblinking gaze.

"I'm sorry?"

"Are you asking me if you're sorry?"

"Um, no, but it's just that…" Lucky's stomach growled. Loudly. "It's just that I didn't want to be late for morning tea."

"Come with me," the headmistress said. As she turned around, Sarah and the other eavesdroppers darted back into the tearoom. Lucky sighed. There'd be no scones today.

The headmistress's office contained lots of lovely things. A collection of china plates graced the walls, lace doilies draped every surface, and a pair of lovebirds twittered in a wicker birdcage.

"How many times have you visited my office this school year?" Madam Barrow asked as she settled into her desk chair.

"I'm not sure." Lucky had lost count.

"Eight times, Miss Prescott. *Eight times.*" Lucky nodded. The incidents streamed through her mind. She'd slid down the entry banister. She'd climbed a ladder to check out a bird's nest on a school windowsill. She'd eaten a cricket on a dare. And there was all the running. "I'm beginning to think that I'm sharing my office with you."

That was a funny thought. Lucky giggled, then tried to take it back but made a snorting sound instead. "Sorry." It was a well-known fact that Madam Barrow did not possess a sense of humor.

The headmistress tapped her fingers on her desk. She seemed more upset than usual, sitting as if a plank were tied to her back. Lucky hadn't been invited to sit, so she stood just inside the doorway, doing her best not to fidget. "This is a finishing school, Miss Prescott. Do you know what that means?"

Of course she did. She'd heard the motto hundreds of times. "Preparing Young Ladies for Society."

"Correct. Young ladies, such as you, enter this school as unformed little lumps of clay. Under my guidance and the tutelage of your teachers, you are shaped—formed—into finished works of art." She smiled, but there was no warmth in the expression.

Lucky didn't like to think of herself as a lump of

clay—or a lump of anything. And she was not quite sure why she had to be turned into a work of art. Works of art were stuck in museums, behind glass or on pedestals. Works of art stayed in one place. That was much worse than being stuck in recitations.

The headmistress opened her desk drawer and took out a piece of writing paper. Then, using her marble pen, she began to write. She paused a moment, glanced up. "You've put me in a difficult position. Are you aware of this?"

"I didn't mean to." Lucky felt a tingle on her ankle, the beginning of a blister. Those shoes were really the worst. Why did every part of her uniform have to be so stiff? She shifted her weight, trying to find relief.

"Are you listening to me?" the headmistress asked.

"Yes." Lucky stopped moving. "I won't run anymore. Really, I won't. I mean, not inside. Unless there's a fire. I have to run if there's a fire. Or an earthquake."

The headmistress sighed. "Miss Prescott, I want all my students to succeed, but I'm beginning to question your chances."

That sounded very serious. Lucky didn't set out to break the rules or to test the headmistress's patience. It just happened. "I know. I'm really sorry. Truly I am. But I saw this cowboy outside and I wanted to…"

Leaving school without a parent or guardian was strictly prohibited, and by admitting this, she'd just made things worse.

The headmistress turned red, as if she'd painted rouge over her entire face. "I find I am near my wits' end. How can I be expected to put up with such continued willfulness?"

Willfulness? Lucky wondered. Was it willful to want to see a real, live cowboy up close? Was it willful to want to get somewhere quickly? Was it willful to want a scone? If so, then why was being willful such a bad thing? The problem, in Lucky's opinion, was that there were too many rules and way too much sitting. She couldn't help that her legs got twitchy.

The headmistress began writing again.

"I didn't mean to bump into you. I'm sorry, I really am." Lucky leaned forward. "What are you writing?"

The headmistress wrote a few more lines, then signed her name with a flourish. After folding the paper, she applied a blob of wax and pressed the school's seal into it. "The question you must ask yourself, Fortuna, is *What am I made of?*" She held out the letter. "Please deliver this to your father after school. You are dismissed."

Lucky reluctantly took the letter and was about to head out the door when the headmistress cleared her throat. *Oh, that's right*, Lucky thought. She turned back around and said, "Thank you, Ma'am." The headmistress nodded. Then Lucky made her escape.

On previous occasions, upon leaving the headmistress's office, Lucky had felt a wave of relief. But never before had the headmistress said she was at her wits' end. And never before had she written a letter with a secret message to Lucky's father. There could be nothing good in that letter.

Fortuna Esperanza Navarro Prescott fought the urge to run as she tucked what she believed to be her doom into her pocket.

2

Lucky stood in the hallway as the other students streamed out of the tearoom. Most greeted her with sympathetic smiles, for Lucky was well liked at school. Only Sarah Nickerson stopped to gloat. "In trouble again? When are you going to realize that you don't belong here?" Sarah asked. But she didn't wait for an answer. Lucky wouldn't have bothered anyway. It was no use trying to talk to someone like Sarah, who'd been taught by her parents that because one side of Lucky's family didn't "come from money," Lucky wasn't Sarah's social equal.

As the hallway cleared, the last student to emerge from the tearoom was Emma Popham. Emma had a sneaky look on her face. She glanced around, then slipped a scone into Lucky's hand. "Thanks," Lucky whispered, then ate the scone in two bites. She and Emma always looked out for each other.

After wiping crumbs off her lips, Lucky grabbed the handles of Emma's rolling chair, a fancy chair with wheels that allowed Emma to move about. As a little girl, Emma had suffered a sickness that left her legs skinny and weak. She could stand for short periods, but she couldn't walk more than a few steps.

"So I heard," Emma said as Lucky wheeled her down the hallway, "you were in the headmistress's office."

"I'm setting a school record."

Emma placed her hands over a pair of books that lay in her lap. "Did Madame Barrow remind you that"—she conjured a British accent for the rest of the sentence—"you're a little lump of clay that needs to be molded into a work of art?"

"Actually, she told me that *you're* the lump."

"No, you are."

"No, you are." They both laughed.

One of the nice things about going to the most prestigious school in the city was that the school came complete with all the latest technologies, including an elevator. Lucky opened the elevator gate, then the door, and pushed Emma into the small chamber before stepping inside behind her. She turned the lever. After a loud clanking sound and a quick jarring motion, the elevator moved slowly upward.

Lucky leaned against the wall. "Madame Barrow wrote a letter to my dad."

"What does it say?"

"I don't know. But I'm guessing it's not good. Something about me being *willful* and having too much *spirited energy*."

"Well, that's better than having a stick up your behind like Sarah," Emma said. "Besides, your dad won't get mad. He never gets mad at you. He adores you." Emma was trying to make Lucky feel better, but Lucky's stomach tightened with worry. She didn't want to disappoint her father. "Why were you late, anyway?"

"I saw a cowboy and a horse with feathers in his mane!"

"Really?"

"Yes, really. Walking down the street. The cowboy was passing out pieces of paper to people and I wanted to see what it was all about."

"Did you get one?"

"No." Though she still wanted answers about the cowboy and his horse, she couldn't shake her worry about the letter. "What if Madame Barrow wants to kick me out of the school?"

"Never," Emma said with a wave of her hand. "She wouldn't do that."

"But what if the letter's really bad and Dad decides I need some kind of punishment?"

Emma shrugged. "It's really not a big deal. If he does punish you, then he'll do what my parents always do. He'll make you stay home on weekends and not go to any—" She gasped. "Oh no. You don't think he'll make you miss *my* party?"

The elevator had reached the third floor, but Lucky didn't open the door right away. Emma's question hung in the air over both their heads, like a storm cloud.

Emma's birthday party was going to be the most glorious party ever. At least that's how Lucky imagined it. The Pophams lived in a stone mansion on Church Street, with a private stable for their carriage horses. No expense would be spared for the event. Emma's perfumed invitations had been mailed weeks ago. "I'm going to your party," Lucky said as she opened the elevator door. "I'll do chores for the rest of my life if I have to. I'll help with the shopping and the cooking. Nothing's going to stop me." She grabbed the handles and wheeled Emma out of the elevator.

"And I'll help you with those chores," Emma said. "Because there's no way I'm turning thirteen without my best friend."

Library was next on the schedule. According to Madame Barrow, young ladies should always take time to properly digest a meal, so after enjoying tea and scones, they faced another long bout of sitting. But Lucky didn't mind, because she loved reading. Adored it, in fact. For a young lady of society, reading was the only socially approved type of exploration.

The school library took up most of the third floor. Bookshelves lined the walls, and embroidered cushions decorated the velvet chairs. A fire usually crackled in the winter, but on this spring day the window was open, permitting a nice breeze. Lucky wheeled Emma to their favorite corner, by a window that overlooked the park. Emma held up the books she'd been cradling on her lap. "Dad got these for us. They're both by Jules Verne. I can't wait to start this one. *Twenty Thousand Leagues Under the Sea.*" She and Lucky were drawn to the same kind of stories—grand adventures in exotic locations, brimming with danger. This was one of the many reasons why they were best friends.

"Oh, I've read that one," Lucky said. "Everyone thinks there's this huge sea monster, and they send out these guys to kill it, but the sea monster turns out to be a—"

"Don't tell me the whole story!" Emma cried.

"Oops." Lucky smiled. "Trust me, you're gonna love it." She grabbed the other book. "*Journey to the Center of the Earth.* This looks great."

"You can keep it."

"Thanks."

The clock struck eleven. The other students found seats, and everyone took out their books and began to read. Along with the clock's ticking and pages rustling, young children squealed in the park, but none of those sounds distracted Lucky. The only time she didn't get squirmy was when her nose was stuck in a book. *How does one get to the center of the earth?* she wondered. Was there a secret tunnel? She'd never been outside the city, except to go to her grandfather's country house upstate. Lucky opened to the first page, ready for another story to take her someplace amazing.

A shadow fell across the page. Mrs. Beachwood, a portly woman with a jiggly chin and a warm smile, had wandered over. "I see you two are sticking with the adventure genre."

"Yes," Emma said.

Was that a twinkle in Mrs. Beachwood's eye? "Wouldn't you prefer a gentler story? A story about taking care of your home?" She held up a book titled *The Joys of Domestic Duties.* Emma and Lucky cringed. "Or perhaps this one?" The second choice was *Manners and Etiquette of a Young Lady.* Because it had been written by the headmistress, it had been read by most of the students. Lucky groaned to herself. The corners of Mrs.

Beachwood's eyes crinkled in amusement. "I see how it is. You'd rather read about dangerous places, courageous heroes, and evil villains than about how to tell a salad fork from a dessert fork."

"Yes!" they both said, forgetting the quiet rule.

Mrs. Beachwood cupped a hand around the side of her mouth and whispered, "Well, I wholly approve." Then she began to shelve books.

Lucky curled up in her chair and opened to the first chapter. She always felt a rush of excitement when she began a new book. Where was she going? What would she see? Would this story give her nightmares or would it make her laugh? She felt restless again, but it wasn't her legs. The feeling came from a deeper place. Lucky didn't fully understand yet, but what she felt at that moment was longing. There are people who never have this feeling, people who are content to stay put. But Lucky longed to go somewhere. Maybe not to the center of the earth, maybe not twenty thousand leagues under the sea, but somewhere.

Somewhere beyond her tidy, inside life.

3

Cora Thayer Prescott rarely left the house without a
black parasol. She highly approved of the practical
device, which was handy in most weather situations.
In case of sun, it protected her fair skin. In case of rain,
snow, or hail, it kept her expensive hats and clothing
dry. The only time she didn't carry one was during a
storm. She'd come to that wise decision after learning
that a distant cousin had been struck by lightning while
carrying a parasol in a hurricane and thus had been
left a bit *befuddled in the brain*. Cora didn't have time
for befuddlement or any kind of impracticality. Today,
however, with the sun gentle and pleasant, Cora's parasol
was tightly folded, ready to be employed in case the
temperature should rise, or droplets of rain should fall.
Spring weather was so unpredictable.

As was this day. Very unpredictable, which annoyed
Cora, for she tried to keep her days in a state of utmost
order. Cora highly approved of routines. Life was messy
and complicated, and the best way to deal with messy and
complicated was to wrap it up in a tight bow. Each day
planned. Each hour scheduled. But she'd received a note

from her younger brother that his housekeeper was ill and unable to meet Lucky after school. Could Cora fetch Lucky? Cora, who'd been in the middle of a meeting of the Ladies' Social Betterment Society, had read the note quickly. Of course her niece could not walk alone. It was improper for young ladies of society to go unescorted on city sidewalks. So she'd politely withdrawn from her meeting and was now making her way toward the school.

As she walked down the sidewalk, her long skirt swishing, her steps were purposeful but not rapid. Cora often added an afternoon walk to her schedule. Walking was appropriate exercise for ladies of society. Expansion of the lungs was most beneficial to a sturdy constitution.

As Cora neared the school, she spotted Lucky standing on the sidewalk, waving as a carriage pulled away. Another girl waved from the carriage window. "See you at my party!" the girl called. Cora vaguely recognized the girl, but when she noticed the rolling chair tucked at the back of the carriage, she remembered that the girl was Lucky's best friend.

"Good-bye, Emma!" Lucky called.

Cora smiled. Her heart always warmed when she saw her niece. Had Lucky grown another inch? How long had it been since they'd been in each other's company? Cora ran through a mental list of activities and realized that she hadn't seen her niece in one month. She supposed it was possible to grow an inch in one month. How quickly time passed. How quickly Lucky was changing. A pang of guilt tugged at her. Perhaps she should make more time for her niece.

Lucky's boots were nicely polished and her hair properly braided. She was such a lovely girl, with a bubbling personality and keen intellect. Under the right guidance, Lucky would grow to be an amazing woman who could do anything she set her mind to. Cora believed it was her duty to be a role model to Lucky, but she was not Lucky's mother. She was her aunt, and she'd been reminded many times that parenting duties and decisions were up to Lucky's father, Jim. As brother and sister, Jim and Cora were polar opposites, and she did not always approve of his laid-back ways. But he was the parent, and it was not her place to interfere.

Though she did, sometimes. Interfere. When she thought it necessary. Being a single parent was a tough job, and Jim didn't like to wear the hat of disciplinarian. Nor had he fully recovered from that sad day, many long years ago, when he'd lost his wife.

"Hello, Lucky," Cora said with a warm smile, pausing just a moment before pulling Lucky in for a quick hug.

Lucky returned the hug, then took a step back. "Aunt Cora? What are you doing here?"

"Mrs. MacFinn is not feeling well. I've come to walk you home."

"Oh." Lucky frowned. Cora frowned, too, worried that her niece wasn't happy to see her. But when Lucky's hands darted behind her back, and her big green eyes looked away, Cora raised an eyebrow.

"Lucky, what are you hiding?" she asked in a hushed voice.

Lucky shuffled in place. Then she revealed a letter. "It's from the headmistress," she mumbled. "For Dad."

Normally, Cora would have told her niece not to mumble, to speak clearly and to hold her head high. "Words matter," she often said, "so make certain your words are clear and delivered with confidence." But in this case, with parents milling about, Cora didn't mind the mumbling. The letter was no business of anyone's. Jim and Lucky would discuss it in the privacy of their home. Cora took the letter and tucked it into her bag.

"Madame Barrow was really mad," Lucky began to explain. "But I was just trying to—"

"This is neither the time nor the place," Cora said. "You can discuss it later." She caught the judgmental stare of a woman she knew all too well—Mrs. Nickerson, wife to the president of the city's largest bank. Cora smiled politely. It was well known that Lucky often had troubles at school, and clearly Mrs. Nickerson had heard about the latest incident, whatever that might be. Mrs. Nickerson turned and spoke to another woman, and even though they kept their voices hushed, Cora heard the words clearly: "She acts wild because she doesn't have a mother."

That comment stabbed Cora right to her heart. She could feel her face heating up, and with every ounce of her being, she wanted to pounce on that woman like a mother lion defending her cub. How *dare* she say such a cruel thing! But this was a public place, and Cora Prescott was not about to make a scene. Instead, she turned her back to Mrs. Nickerson, reached out, and straightened Lucky's straw hat. The ribbon was beginning to fray and needed replacing. This was the kind of thing Lucky's father would never notice, but was important nonetheless. "Let's go."

Lucky walked fast. She'd get ahead of Cora, then backtrack. She'd clearly inherited her energy from her father. Cora remembered many occasions when Jim had gotten in trouble at school, and a few times when he'd brought home a letter from his school's headmaster. *Like father, like daughter*, Cora thought bemusedly. Perhaps she could help find a good physical outlet for Lucky's energy. She'd look into tennis lessons at the club. Tennis was a civilized form of exercise. As the saying went, *sound body, sound mind.* She'd bring up the subject with Jim as soon as possible.

The city was in its usual state of busyness. Horse-drawn carriages and wagons crowded the road. Men in suits and bowler hats and women in high-collared jackets and long skirts strolled the sidewalks, shopping and conversing. There were vendors hawking their wares and stray cats meowing from alleys. And there were the odors—the musky scent of horses (of which Cora was not fond) and chimney smoke. But pleasant odors lingered as well, like chickens roasting in a butcher's shop, and a bakery with apple cake just out of the oven. "Those sweets will spoil your appetite," Cora said when Lucky stared longingly into the bakery window.

"Extra, extra, read all about it! Gold found out West!" a newsboy called. Cora stopped to buy a paper.

"What if we don't give the letter to Dad?" Lucky asked, after Cora had paid the newsboy a nickel and handed the paper to her to carry. "What if we accidentally lose it?"

Cora didn't ask Lucky what she'd done. The letter was specifically addressed to Mr. Jim Prescott, and if Cora got involved, she might be accused of interfering again. She was curious, of course. But she knew it was probably the same thing—that Lucky had been in the wrong place at the wrong time, drawn there by her curiosity and energy. "Whether your actions are good or bad, you must own your responsibility," Cora said, taking advantage of a teaching moment. "We learn not from success but from failure. Look your father in the eyes, admit your wrongdoing, and you will grow and learn."

"Fine." Lucky's shoulders slumped. "Are you mad at me because I got in trouble again?"

"I'm not *mad* at you. I love you with all my heart. You do know that, don't you?"

Lucky nodded. They began walking again. But Cora couldn't shake the image of Mrs. Nickerson's disapproving eye. "I am, however, *concerned*. I don't think your father has conveyed to you the importance of these school years." Cora gently guided Lucky so they made a wide berth around a man and his ornery-looking bulldog. "The girls at Madame Barrow's are your social peers. They are the ones who will be inviting you to parties, to dances, and as you grow up, to weddings. They are *your people*. The headmistress has influence, here and abroad. If you are in her good graces you can expect to be included on many invitation lists."

"I don't care about invitation lists. The only party I care about is Emma's birthday." Lucky frowned. "I really hope Dad lets me go."

Cora doubted her brother would keep his only daughter from her best friend's birthday. When it came to discipline, Jim was as softhearted as a stuffed animal. She'd never even heard him raise his voice. But rather than set her niece at ease, Cora decided that a bit of worry might be good for Lucky. "Perhaps next time you will think about consequences before you act." Cora stopped outside a hat shop. "I have something to pick up. Are you coming in?"

"I'd rather wait out here," Lucky said.

It would be easier to have Lucky remain outside. When made to wait inside a store, Lucky could be the proverbial "bull in a china shop."

"Very well. I'll be only a few minutes." Cora stepped inside. The woman at the counter greeted her, then collected the blue wool hat that Cora had ordered. It bore a pheasant feather and would look quite smart with her coat. As she paid for the hat, she noticed the selection of ribbons and chose a new one for Lucky's straw hat. Then, hatbox in hand, she emerged from the shop.

Lucky was gone.

Cora's heart skipped a beat. She told herself not

to panic. She knew her niece had simply wandered, distracted by something, and was nearby. But where? She glanced up and down the sidewalk.

Perhaps she should have told Lucky to stay put. But Lucky should know that rule by now. With a determined jut of her chin, Cora tucked her parasol beneath her arm. It was one thing to try to keep a schedule in place, but trying to keep Lucky in place was as impossible as trying to contain a breeze.

A breeze with a braid.

4

Lucky waved apologetically at a driver as he hollered, "Watch out!" and his horse reared to avoid running over her. She should have looked both ways before darting into the road, but something had caught her eye. And she couldn't miss out, not again!

It was the beautiful black horse, the one with the red blanket and feathers in his mane, and the same cowboy she'd seen earlier, only this time the cowboy was riding the horse. She wanted to call out to them, but they were too far away to hear her above the city noise. The cowboy rode around the corner, disappearing from view.

With one hand atop her straw hat to keep it in place, and the rolled newspaper in her other hand, Lucky skidded to a stop to avoid another carriage. She waited for it to pass, then hurried onto the sidewalk. She picked up her pace, scurrying between pedestrians. Why were they walking so slowly? She dashed around a couple strolling arm in arm, then dodged a woman with a basket of flowers. "Excuse me. Excuse me." She bumped into a young deliveryman carrying parcels of laundry. "Sorry." She leaped over a crate and nearly overturned a small fruit stand, sending an apple rolling. She grabbed the wayward fruit, plopped it back into its bin, then hurried away before the shopkeeper could holler at her.

As she rounded the corner, she nearly squealed with glee. There they were! The cowboy and his horse had stopped at an ornamental fountain, from which the horse was taking a long drink. One final dash and Lucky was at the horse's side. A few other kids joined her and began petting the horse. He was leaner and more graceful than the draft horses that pulled city wagons. He didn't seem to mind all the attention.

"What's his name?" Lucky asked.

The cowboy tipped back his hat, revealing his face. Lucky gasped. It wasn't a cowboy after all. "His name's Shadow," the cowgirl replied. "He's the best jumping horse this side of the Mississippi, or any side of the Mississippi for that matter." She smiled at Lucky. "Come see us perform tonight at our Wild West show."

"What's a Wild West show?" Lucky asked.

"What's a Wild West show?" The cowgirl reached into her saddlebag and pulled out a piece of paper. It was a small flyer advertising the show. "Why, it's the gosh-darned best thing you could ever see. We got rough riders and rope slingers. We got stagecoach robbers and six-shooters." Lucky didn't know what those were, but they sounded exciting. "We got Deadeye Dave, the fastest draw in the West. He can shoot a bull's-eye blindfolded."

"That's impossible," a gentleman said. A small crowd had begun to gather. Lucky wasn't the only one who found a cowgirl in the middle of the city to be an unusual sight.

"You calling me a liar?" the cowgirl asked, sitting up straight in her saddle. "I don't make this stuff up, mister. It's impossible for most people to hit a bull's-eye blindfolded, but Deadeye Dave hits it every time." She raised her voice so those passing by could hear. "Come see for yourself. You can watch Wild Bill ride a bull, right up on the stage. And Shadow and I will jump through a ring of fire!" The crowd murmured in disbelief. "And we open the show with a horse parade. We got fancy horses from all over the world. You can't miss that!" She slid out of the saddle, then handed Lucky a flyer.

"Ring of fire?" Lucky asked, trying to imagine what that would look like. "Isn't that dangerous for your horse?"

The cowgirl ran her hand along Shadow's neck. "I'd never put Shadow into danger. Me and him, well, we're like brother and sister. We look out for each other." She leaned close and whispered, "Don't you worry. The fire's a trick. An *illusion*." She winked.

While the cowgirl talked to some of the other onlookers, Lucky read the flyer.

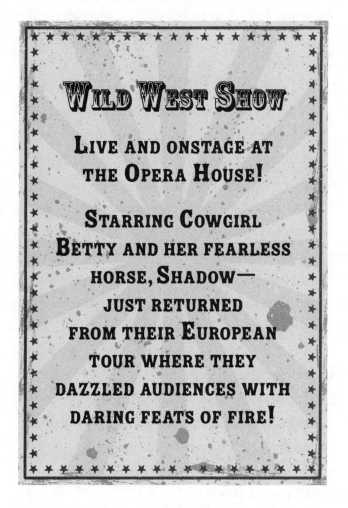

WILD WEST SHOW

LIVE AND ONSTAGE AT THE OPERA HOUSE!

STARRING COWGIRL BETTY AND HER FEARLESS HORSE, SHADOW— JUST RETURNED FROM THEIR EUROPEAN TOUR WHERE THEY DAZZLED AUDIENCES WITH DARING FEATS OF FIRE!

The crowd began to disperse. But Lucky lingered. She had so many questions. "Are you Cowgirl Betty?" Betty nodded eagerly. "You've been to Europe?"

"Yep, that ocean crossing was no fun, I'll tell you that. Shadow and I, we like our feet on solid ground." Lucky tried to imagine a horse riding on a ship. Did he stay up on deck? Did he have his own cabin? Shadow snorted. Then he bumped Lucky's hand with his muzzle. "Aw, look at that. He wants you to pet him. Go on. He's real nice."

Lucky placed her palm on Shadow's muzzle, finding the soft, velvety part around his nostrils. His breath was warm. She wanted to pet him forever.

"There you are!" Aunt Cora hurried up to Lucky. "You scared the daylights out of me. What were you thinking, crossing the road without an escort? You could have been run over!" She set her hatbox on the edge of the fountain, then dabbed her face with her handkerchief as she tried to catch her breath.

"Sorry," Lucky said. "But look at this." She showed the flyer to Cora. "Can we go?"

Cora pursed her lips. "I should think not."

"But it's at the opera house. We always go to the opera house."

"Yes, to see the ballet, the symphony, and the opera. Not a *Wild West* show."

"But…"

"Fortuna Esperanza Navarro Prescott, a show like that is not appropriate for young ladies. Too wild, too loud, full of hooligans and roughhousers. I don't want to hear another word about it. Now give that back." She turned and hurried back to the fountain, where some pigeons were roosting on her hatbox. "Shoo! Shoo!"

Lucky reluctantly handed the flyer to Betty. "Maybe next time," she said sadly.

Shadow pressed his muzzle into Lucky's hand. "He sure likes you," Betty noticed. "Since you can't come to the show, do you want to ride him?"

"Really?" Surprised by the invitation, Lucky took a step back. "But I don't know how to ride."

"That's okay. I'll show you." Cowgirl Betty patted the saddle. Lucky had often imagined herself sitting on a horse's back. "He's real easy to ride. He won't buck. Come on; it'll be fun."

A few other kids began to jump up and down. "Can I ride him? Huh? Can I ride him?" they pleaded.

"I only got time to let one of you take a ride. And this young lady here is the one Shadow chose. Come on, get on up."

Lucky tapped the rolled newspaper against her leg. Certainly it would be an adventure to ride a horse for the very first time. She looked over her shoulder. Aunt Cora was still over at the fountain, busily folding her handkerchief, and adjusting her hat, and straightening this and that to somehow make herself even more presentable. If Lucky got up on that saddle, super quick, Cora wouldn't be able to stop her.

"Yes, I'd really like to ride him." Lucky lifted her foot, preparing to set it into the stirrup.

"Lucky!" In a burst of uncharacteristic speed, Cora rushed to Lucky's side. "What are you doing?"

"She's gonna take a little ride on old Shadow here," Betty explained. "It won't be dangerous. Shadow won't take off with her. He's never done that before." She paused. "Well, there was that one time. The kid was a bit upset, on account he ended up so far from home, but everything worked out just fine in the end."

"Sounds perfectly safe to me," Lucky said, but she knew Cora wouldn't budge.

"Horses are not perfectly safe." Cora placed a protective arm around Lucky's shoulder. "Good day," she said to Cowgirl Betty. She collected her hatbox, then led Lucky away.

A few moments later they were back on the sidewalk, walking beneath Aunt Cora's parasol. "How could you possibly think I would let you ride a horse?" Cora asked, her nose higher in the air than usual. "I think you've gotten too much sun today."

Lucky didn't argue. She'd already gotten into enough trouble today. But as they headed toward home, Lucky glanced over her shoulder. No cowgirl or horse in sight, as if they'd been figments of her imagination. But Lucky could still smell that musky horse scent, deep within her nostrils.

Deep within her soul.

5

When Lucky and Cora arrived at Lucky's house, Mr. MacFinn, the aged butler, took their hats and coats, and the hatbox and parasol. Lucky set the newspaper on the table for her father. He liked to read it right after supper. Cora took the dreaded letter from her purse and set it beside the newspaper. Lucky glared at the wax seal. Oh, how she wanted to toss that letter into the rubbish bin!

The housekeeper, Mrs. MacFinn, was in bed with sniffles, and since sniffles were nothing to mess around with, Cora heated up some broth and brought it to her. She mixed in a spoonful of medicinal tonic, just to be safe. Then she sent Mr. MacFinn down the street to purchase a cold roast chicken and potato salad from a delicatessen. The long dining room table was used only for dinner parties, so Lucky and Cora set the smaller table in the dining nook. "We may be having a picnic for dinner, but I find that even simple food tastes better when served on china," Cora said as she set three porcelain dishes onto the damask tablecloth. Lucky placed a silver fork and silver knife on the right side of the plate. "The fork goes on the left," Cora corrected.

"And always place the silverware in an even line, one inch from the end of the table."

Having Cora over for dinner was no fun at all. It was like being under a microscope. "Aunt Cora, you don't have to stay. I can wait for Dad by myself."

"Nonsense. I'm happy to stay." And with that, Cora bustled into the kitchen to get water glasses. Lucky sighed. It was going to be a long night of lectures, no doubt about it.

Mr. MacFinn returned with the food. Cora made him a plate and excused him to enjoy his meal in the kitchen. Lucky lit a pair of candles, for both she and her father loved candlelight. Then she paced along the Persian carpet, her gaze flitting between the headmistress's letter and the front door. The grandfather clock struck six. "I wonder what's keeping Dad?" she asked.

"Here I am!" Jim Prescott announced as he flung open the front door. He hugged Lucky so hard he lifted her off the ground.

"Dad, I can't breathe," she said with a groan, but she hugged him back equally hard. He always smelled like the office—a mixture of ink and papers, dust and tobacco. His mustache tickled the side of her neck. Mr. MacFinn, a napkin tucked into his collar, strode out of the kitchen and took Jim's bowler hat and overcoat.

"Cora, my dear sister!"

Cora squeaked as Jim's arms wrapped around her. "Honestly, Jim, I don't see why you must hug like that. You are *not* a bear." She stepped back and smoothed her blouse. "You've wrinkled me."

"And I love you, too," he said with a laugh. "Thank you for escorting Lucky home. I know I interrupted your busy schedule."

"No thank-you is necessary. I was happy to do it."

"You're late," Lucky said to her father as they walked to the dining nook.

"I didn't mean to worry you," he said, running a hand through his dark blond hair. "The paperwork was piling up. We've got that new line out West, the one that's expanding all the way to the ocean. It's exciting, but it's the longest line we've built." Jim worked at JP & Sons, a railroad started by his father, James Prescott Sr. "Hey, this looks great," he said, grabbing a seat. "I'm famished!"

Lucky was famished, too, having eaten nothing since lunch. She and her father dug right in. Cora pursed her lips. "Eating so quickly is not good for the digestion. Lucky, stop swinging your legs, please. And don't you two ever use napkins?" Jim grabbed his napkin, stuck out his pinkie, and delicately dabbed the corners of his mouth. Then he winked at Lucky. The only time they ever got lectures about manners was when Cora came to visit.

When the meal was finished, Cora made coffee. Jim took a sip, then sat back in his chair. "Why are you two staring at me? Do I have potato salad on my face?"

Cora glanced at Lucky. It was time to deal with the letter. "Uh, Dad," Lucky said, squirming in her chair as though it were covered in fire ants. "I get to go to Emma's party, right?"

"Sure."

"No matter what, I get to go?"

"Uh-huh."

"Do you promise? No matter what happens?"

His blue eyes crinkled with amusement. "And what might happen, pray tell?"

Cora folded her hands and set them on the table. Lucky could practically read her aunt's thoughts—*look him in the eye, hold your head high, and admit your wrongdoing.*

Lucky pushed her braid behind her shoulder, then sat up straight. "I got caught running again, inside the school, but this time I bumped right into the headmistress." Cora cringed. "Oh, and we both landed on our backsides."

Jim raised an eyebrow. Cora groaned.

"I'm sorry. I'll help Mrs. MacFinn and do extra chores all week, or for the rest of my life if you want me to, just so I can still go to Emma's party."

"Well, that sounds like a good plan." He seemed satisfied. "Where's my newspaper?"

"Jim!" Cora scolded.

Jim cleared his throat. "Yes, of course. Lucky, no more running in school. Okay?" She nodded. "Good, now let's talk about something else, shall we?"

Lucky would have been delighted to talk about something else, but Cora tilted her head toward the letter. Slowly, as if walking to a guillotine, Lucky collected the letter, then set it before her father. "This is for you."

Jim broke the wax seal. His gaze glided across the words. Lucky hoped her father would read it aloud, so she could hear all the mean and rotten things the headmistress had written about her. *Rule-Breaker. Willful. Unformed Lump.* "Is it bad?" she asked.

Jim peered over the top of the white linen paper. "Madame Barrow feels that you are possessed with an abnormal amount of spirited energy, and that I should send you to a physician for inspection and possible treatment." Lucky went rigid. What did that mean? What kind of treatment? Foreboding silence filled the room as Lucky imagined herself being pricked with needles and made to drink cod liver oil or something equally disgusting.

The silence was broken by Jim's belly laugh.

"Jim!" Cora said. "I don't see what is so funny. This is a serious matter. The headmistress believes there is something wrong with Lucky."

He stopped laughing and turned serious. "Do *you* think there's something wrong with Lucky?"

"Of course not! She's a Prescott. But the headmistress has the power to send Lucky to..." Cora could barely say the words. "To a less-prestigious school."

Jim faced his daughter. "Lucky, do you promise you will try harder to follow the rules?"

"Yes, I will."

"Then that's good enough for me." He crumpled the letter and tossed it over his shoulder.

Relief washed over Lucky. That letter had been weighing on her all day. She felt so light, she thought she might float right out of the room. Emma would be so happy to hear the news.

"I'm not sure this matter has been settled," Cora said, but she didn't get to continue that thought, because she was interrupted by insistent knocking.

"Who could that be?" Jim asked.

They all turned to watch as Mr. MacFinn scurried past. He opened the front door and said, "Good evening, sir, may I take your coat?"

"I must speak to my son right away! Urgent business, I tell you! Where is he?"

"But, sir, may I take your hat?"

"Didn't you hear me? This business cannot wait!"

6

The bellowing voice belonged to Lucky's grandfather,
James Prescott Sr. Lucky's heart sank. Such a late,
unexpected visit could mean only one thing—the
headmistress must have contacted him. This was a
terrible turn of events, because James Sr. was even more
opinionated than Cora.

Even in his old age, James Sr. was a towering figure.
In his youth, he'd been blond, like his children, but his
thick muttonchops and mustache were now white.

"Father, what brings you here at this hour?" Jim
asked. He reached out and shook his father's hand.
Things were always very formal with James Sr.

"Matters of importance," James Sr. said. While his body
was aging, his blue eyes remained bright and focused, like
a bird of prey. "Lucky, my dearest granddaughter," he said,
reaching out to give her a pat on the head.

"Hi, Grandpa." The scent of pipe tobacco lingered on
his wool clothing.

"You're getting bigger every time I see you. Must
be all of Mrs. MacFinn's good cooking." Lucky nodded.
"And how are things at school?"

Was he waiting for her confession? Maybe she should get the unpleasantness over and apologize right away. "Grandpa, I ran into—"

"Wonderful," he said with a brisk clap. "Now, your father and I have business to attend to. We need to discuss the railroad."

Jim led James Sr. into the parlor, a cozy room with velvet-covered furniture and a small fireplace. Cora and Lucky followed. James Sr. grimaced as he sat on the divan. Though he appeared robust in health, he'd mentioned some aches of late. "Darn this rheumatism. Getting old is no picnic in the park, that's for sure." Jim poured James Sr. some coffee. Lucky, Cora, and Jim all sat, waiting for the Prescott patriarch to speak. After a few sips, James Sr. explained his unexpected visit. "One hour ago, I received a telegram from Miradero. The project manager is dead."

"Dead?" Cora's hand flew to her heart.

"Stone cold. Fell off a ledge while scouting territory."

"Oh dear. Lucky, cover your ears," Cora said.

Lucky didn't cover her ears. This was good stuff, right out of an adventure novel.

"Did he have an assistant?" Jim asked. "Who's going to take over?"

"That's why I'm here, Son. You're going to take over."

"Me?" Jim's eyes widened with surprise. "But I can't manage the project from here. I'd have to move to Miradero."

"Exactly so. And I need you to leave right away." James Sr. said this in a very matter-of-fact way, for he expected his orders to be followed. "Tomorrow."

Lucky wasn't sure if she'd heard correctly. "Wait. What did you say?"

James Sr. set his coffee aside. "There's no way around it, Jim. You are the very best option."

Cora cleared her throat, making a silent point that James Sr. did have another option, someone equally capable, but being a daughter in this day and age meant that she wasn't even considered.

Jim stood and started pacing. "Father, I'm happy to help out. I'll go to Miradero and begin the hiring process for a new manager. That shouldn't take long. A few weeks, maybe, a month at the most. Cora can come here and stay with Lucky while I'm gone."

"Of course," Cora said.

A month with Aunt Cora? That would mean a bath *every* day, vitamin tonics, and evening lectures about culture. Lucky held back a groan.

James Sr. shook his head. "You won't be hiring anyone. *You* are the new manager. This is a huge project. We've invested everything. We can't afford any delays. If this project fails, the future of JP & Sons is at stake."

Jim stopped pacing. "But that means…"

Lucky jumped to her feet. "We're moving to Miradero? Tomorrow? But…" Her head was spinning. Where was Miradero? What about her friends? What about Emma's party? "But…"

Cora also stood. "Father, you can't mean that Lucky is to move out West?" She wrapped an arm around Lucky's shoulder. "Surely you can't send her to that wild place. She must stay here, in the city, where she's safe and can continue her education."

"Of course I'm not sending my granddaughter out West. Do you think I've gone daft?" James Sr. asked. Lucky felt Cora's arm relax. "I agree that the West is too wild and dangerous for a young girl. Lucky's health and safety are my highest priorities."

Jim frowned. "You expect me to move across the country without my daughter?"

"No," Lucky said, sliding away from Cora and tightly grabbing her father's hand. "I won't stay here without my dad!"

James Sr. slowly rose to his feet. Then his voice

boomed, commanding the attention of everyone, including Mr. and Mrs. MacFinn, who'd been eavesdropping from the other room. "No granddaughter of mine is going to live in the wilderness!" No one said a word, for James Sr. was as inflexible as one of the iron rails that had built his fortune. "Lucky will stay here, and that is final!"

7

Lucky wrapped a quilt around her shoulders and sat in the darkness of her bedroom, trying to fight back tears. She'd been sent upstairs so the adults could talk about her *in private*, but she could clearly hear their voices. A battle of wills had erupted in the parlor; tempers seemed as hot as the flames in the fireplace.

"Will you two listen to me for once? Leaving the city might be good for her," Jim argued. "The West will give her space to run and explore. She won't be cooped up in that uppity school."

"That *uppity* school costs me a small fortune!" James Sr. bellowed. "I'm giving my granddaughter the best education money can buy."

"Jim, be rational," Cora pleaded. "I know you don't want to leave without Lucky, but think of all the dangers out there. How can you supervise her and take care of her if you have a railroad to build? Surely that will require all your time and attention. What's a young girl to do, alone in such a savage wilderness?"

"Exactly so," James Sr. agreed.

"She won't be alone," Jim said. "I'm her family and that's where she belongs."

"We are also her family and she also belongs with us. I won't hear any more of this nonsense! The West is no place for a young lady." This statement was followed by the stomp of a boot. "She stays!"

"She's my daughter," Jim said. "I'm the one who'll make the decision."

"She's my niece and I'm looking out for her best interests."

"She's my granddaughter and my word is the law in this family!"

Despite the warmth building beneath the quilt, Lucky shivered. Her fate was being batted back and forth like a ball in a tennis match. Stay. Go. Stay. Go. And she didn't have a say in the matter. Whom did she belong to? Who had the right to decide her future? After a few more heated words, the arguing stopped. The front door slammed. Lucky shuffled to the window and peered down at the street. Streetlamps cast a yellowish glow upon James Sr.'s overcoat as he stormed to his waiting coach. Aunt Cora followed close behind, hatbox swinging from her hand. Once they were seated, the driver gave a flick of the reins, and Daisy, the old Prescott mare, began to pull the carriage down the street. Lucky watched until it disappeared from view.

She was desperate to run downstairs and ask her

father what was going to happen tomorrow morning. But for the first time in her memory, Lucky didn't feel like running. She curled tighter into the quilt, as if the cotton batting could protect her. As if the tight and perfect stitches, placed there by her grandmother years ago, could hold her world together. Was she going with her father to a new and dangerous place, or was she staying in her comfortable, civilized world without him? The answer frightened her. James Prescott Sr. was a powerful man, and she'd never heard of him losing an argument.

Jim didn't come upstairs, not for a long while. Lucky's eyelids grew heavy, but she didn't allow herself to drift off to sleep. She reached out and picked up the framed photo she kept beside her bed—the one she looked at every night before going to sleep.

In the photo, a man and a woman stood side by side, holding a baby. It was Lucky's favorite photo of her father and her mother, Milagro. She'd stared at her mother's face countless times. She and Milagro shared the same skin tone and the same dark hair. But people often said that Lucky took after her father. Surely she'd inherited more of her mother than just coloring. Surely she took after her mother in some other way. But how?

"Lucky?" A soft knock on the door startled her. The door creaked open a bit. "Are you awake?"

"Yes."

Jim entered the room. "Your aunt bought this for you." He placed the hat ribbon on the dresser, then sat on the edge of Lucky's bed. His usual cheerfulness was faded, as if the argument with James Sr. had drained him. "Lucky, I—"

He'd come to deliver news, and, clearly, it was bad. Lucky was too angry to cry. She clenched her fists and said the only word she could muster, "No!"

"Lucky, sweetheart, it's going to be okay."

"You're leaving me! How can that be okay?"

"Just listen…" He tried to hug her but she pushed away. The quilt tangled around her legs as she moved to the other side of the room.

"I'm not staying here without you. You can't leave me here. You can't!"

"Please listen to me."

Her anger turned to desperation. "Don't take the job, Dad. Have someone else do it. Tell Grandpa you're not feeling well. That you're sick. Tell him you're dying if you have to. Just don't go!"

"I wish it were that simple. But if JP & Sons doesn't complete this project, we'll go belly-up. We'll lose everything. Do you understand?"

Lucky understood. There'd been a girl at Madame

Barrow's whose family had "lost everything" because the father had gambled away his fortune in a series of card games. The poor girl had to leave school. No one knew where she lived now. There was a rumor she'd been seen in one of the tenement houses, in the bad part of town.

Of course, Lucky didn't want her grandfather to lose the business he'd built. JP & Sons was an immense source of pride. Their railroad laid tracks that carried people across the vast continent, to new homes, to new jobs, to new opportunities. What used to take months of dangerous travel now took only days.

"But Grandpa doesn't want me to go."

"He's only trying to protect you. The town of Miradero is way out West. It's a fairly new town with a small population. And your aunt Cora is right; the frontier is not a safe place. It's full of wild, dangerous animals, and dangerous people, too."

Lucky scowled. "Aunt Cora thinks everything is dangerous."

"Both your aunt and grandfather believe you should continue to live here. This has been your home for most of your life. Your friends are here, your family is—"

"*You're* my family!" Lucky couldn't hold back her tears. The quilt dropped to the floor as she crumpled onto the bed, her face pressed into her pillow. Lucky wasn't prone to tears. The last time she remembered crying was last summer, when she'd broken a toe. But this was a different sort of crying—it came from a much deeper place.

A moment later, her muffled sobbing was interrupted by laughter. "Lucky, you're not letting me speak," Jim said. Lucky raised her head and glared at him. Why did he sound so happy all of a sudden? "You're getting all worked up, and I haven't even told you what I came up here to say." He laughed again. "You're coming with me."

"What?" Had she heard correctly?

"There's no way I'd go without you. Never. We're a team, you and I. And your mother, rest her soul, would never forgive me if I left you."

Lucky threw herself at him. With her arms wrapped around his shoulders, she buried her face in his neck. The tears kept coming, but this time they were happy tears. "Thank you."

After she'd dried her eyes and Jim had dried a few tears, too, they gazed at a poster that was mounted on the wall. The focal point of the poster was a young woman balancing on one leg atop a horse. Her long brown hair flowed behind her. The poster read: EL CIRCO DOS GRILLOS STARRING MILAGRO NAVARRO. This was Lucky's mother, and

Navarro was her maiden name. The horse had ribbons in its mane, and Milagro wore a lovely dress and a pair of brown-and-red cowboy boots that were decorated with flames running up the sides. "Would you like me to tell you the story?" Jim asked.

Lucky nodded. She wasn't a baby anymore, so there was no need for bedtime stories, but this one was special. This story didn't have sea monsters or underwater submersibles or trips to the center of the earth. This story was about her mother, and that's why it was her favorite.

"When I was a young man," Jim began, as he always did, "I told my father that I wanted to leave home and seek adventure. He wasn't very happy about my decision, as he wanted me to get started working in the family business right away. But I had made up my mind, so he bade me good-bye." Lucky used to wonder why her grandfather hadn't just asked Aunt Cora to work in the family business instead. But she'd come to learn that, while working in the family business was acceptable and expected of the men in the Prescott family, it had never been so for the women.

"I didn't have a plan. I had some money in my pocket, some extra clothes in a bag, but the whole world was open to me. Should I hop a ship and travel across the ocean to a new world? Or should I go out West where a wilder adventure lay, ripe for the picking?"

The rest of the story went as follows. Jim had heard the tales of gold, but those were not of much interest to him, for he'd grown up with riches. There were tales of careers to be made in the fur trade, but he couldn't quite imagine himself killing creatures for money. But then he saw an advertisement. Cattle ranchers were looking for ranch hands and were willing to train the new hires. *Cowboys*, they were called. The job required long days in the saddle and long nights under the open sky. The pay was decent, but the applicant had to have his own horse and saddle.

So Jim rode a JP & Sons train out West, bought himself a horse and saddle, and landed a job at a cattle ranch. The Corral, as it was called, was owned by a nice older couple. They kept a few hundred steer that needed watching over. Riding wasn't as easy as it looked. Jim ended up with saddle sores and some pulled muscles, but he eventually got the hang of it. He didn't mind the simple food—beans, potatoes, biscuits, and always plenty of beef. And he didn't mind the long hours of work. There was the occasional danger of a cattle rustler, but for the most part the cowboy life was quiet—crickets in the morning, banjo in the evening. So different from the life of privilege he'd lived, where he had to dress in his waistcoat for dinner and dance on weekends with the daughters of wealthy families.

All was going quite well for Jim until they drove the cattle to auction.

The auction took place in the town of Winslow. There was a lot of time to kill while waiting for the auction to begin, so after securing the cattle in a pen, Jim and the other cowboys headed over to a circus tent to watch the show. A spider monkey handed out tickets and a parrot told everyone, "Show's gonna start. Show's gonna start." Jim and his fellow cowboys got seats in the front row. For the most part, Jim enjoyed watching the acrobats, magicians, and jugglers. But then a young woman rode on horseback to the center of the ring. Jim perched on the edge of his seat. She was the most beautiful girl he'd ever seen. When their eyes met, he forgot how to breathe.

Lucky always thought that part of the story was a little corny. But she also secretly liked it.

The circus ringmaster, a gentleman in a tuxedo, hollered to the crowd, "Ladies and gentlemen, feast your eyes on the magnificent Milagro! Such dangerous feats of daring you have never seen. Watch and be amazed!" The crowd hushed as Milagro began to ride slowly around the ring. Suspenseful music arose from the corner, where a man played the organ. With astonished gazes, the crowd watched as Milagro stood upon her horse's back. Around and around they went, Milagro balancing perfectly, a smile on her face. Then, as the music reached a crescendo, she jumped into the air, did a backflip, and landed gracefully on the ground. The onlookers broke into wild applause. Jim was so enamored, he forgot to clap.

Even though the other cowboys teased him about being lovestruck, he waited after the show to meet Milagro.

"The night I met your mother was the luckiest night of my life," Jim said as he tucked Lucky into bed.

Even though she knew the answer, she asked anyway. "Why was it the luckiest night of your life?"

"Because if I'd never met her, I'd never have you." He kissed her forehead. "You'd better get some sleep. We'll have to get up bright and early to pack for our adventure."

Lucky couldn't believe this was happening. A real adventure, just as she'd longed for. But this was all so quick. While her head began to fill with all sorts of questions, her eyelids grew heavier and heavier. She yawned. "Okay. Night."

As her father left the room, Lucky turned toward the

window. A few stars twinkled. A sliver of moon hung above the street, looking as if someone had taken a bite out of it. And that's exactly how her heart felt, too. She was going with her father, but she was leaving the only place she'd ever called home.

8

The stallion lay beneath the starry sky. This was not the time of the full moon, so the prairie was hidden in darkness. A wolf howled in the distance, but not close enough to bring concern. Some of the herd were asleep, others merely resting. The stallion's sister slept nearby.

It had been a perfect day. During grazing, they'd found a lovely patch of dandelions, a real treat. Bees had also found the flowers, but that didn't stop the stallion. While the others trod cautiously, the stallion impatiently plunged in, pulling the dandelions with his teeth, roots and all. The flowers were so delicious, he didn't mind the few stings on his ankles. This was the herd's favorite time of year, for the tender grasses were plentiful—not as in winter, when dry shrubs and tree bark kept them fed.

This time of year, with mountain snow melting, water was also plentiful. It filled the rivers and branched into smaller streams. It spilled into ponds and creeks, attracting all sorts of critters. For the stallion, there was always something interesting to find along the riverbank—a family of rabbits or a fox den. The streams were a great place for games of chase, which the younger horses enjoyed, especially when they were splashing through water.

There was great joy in the spring. The days were simple—graze, sip water, run, and play.

And sleep.

The stallion's eyelids felt heavy. The contented, deep breaths of the herd were like a lullaby. He folded his front legs and rested his head. As a sliver of moon appeared in the sky, the stallion closed his eyes and drifted into the happy depths of sleep.

Tomorrow would be a new day. And a new adventure.

Part Two

9

Despite feeling under the weather, Mrs. MacFinn insisted on making a special bon voyage breakfast of French toast with maple syrup. She sniffled the entire time, half due to her cold and half due to the emotions of the situation. She'd look at Lucky, then choke back a sob. "I'm not dying," Lucky reminded her.

"Aye, lassie, bless yer sweet soul tha not be tha case. But what will I be doin' without you and Mr. Prescott to watch over?"

Mrs. MacFinn was a nice lady, and Lucky was sorry to upset her. "Why don't you come with us?" Lucky asked.

"And who'll be watching over Mr. MacFinn if I go wit ya? I cannae be leavin' him on his own, now, can I?"

Years ago, the MacFinns had traveled all the way from Scotland. The sea voyage had been a terrible time, with sickness and disease making their way around the ship. Some of the travelers didn't survive. Upon setting foot in this new land, Mr. MacFinn was so grateful to be alive that he swore to himself and his wife that he'd never go anywhere again. Jim had tried his best to persuade Mr. MacFinn to join them on the new frontier, arguing that train travel was quicker and far less dangerous than sea travel. But Mr. MacFinn said he never went back on an oath. It was too bad, really, because Mrs. MacFinn made the best French toast and scrumptious meat pies. Jim told Lucky that the MacFinns were probably better off staying in the city since they were getting quite old and were comfortable with their daily routines. Such dramatic change would be unsettling for them.

Unsettled was exactly how Lucky felt that morning. She swallowed one last bite of toast, then yawned. She'd spent the night fretting and tossing with such vigor that the pillows and quilt had ended up on the floor. With the first ray of dawn, she'd given up trying to sleep, slid out of bed, and began packing. She had no idea how long she'd be in Miradero or what kind of weather to expect, so she decided she might as well take all her clothes. Except for the school uniform. Good riddance!

Two trunks were stuffed to the brim, and she had to sit on them to get them closed and latched. The third trunk she filled with personal items—her grooming supplies, including her alabaster brush and hair ribbons. She selected some of her art supplies—a set of pencils and a book of paper. She wasn't the best artist in the world, but she liked drawing, and it would be something to do during the long train ride. She picked up the photo of her mom and dad and wrapped a scarf around it to protect it from scratches. Then she took the framed poster off the wall, wrapped it in her grandmother's quilt, and set it into the trunk.

She stood in front of her bookshelf.

There was very little room left in the last trunk. How could she leave her beloved books behind? Would there be a bookstore or a library in Miradero? She hoped so. She'd spent countless hours reading about adventurers who set forth into the unknown. Those tales had always seemed so exciting, but now that the unknown was staring Lucky in the face, she wished she could just turn the page or close the cover and make it go away. But this wasn't a story. It was her life. She sighed and grabbed the book Emma had given her.

Emma.

A wave of sadness washed over Lucky. Picking and choosing which items to leave behind was difficult, certainly, but leaving behind a best friend was almost unbearable. She and Emma had grown up together. They'd spent every school day together. They'd shared secrets and laughter. And tears. But there was no time to say good-bye in person. Emma lived way across town. A deep ache settled in the pit of Lucky's stomach.

While Jim finished his packing, Lucky wrote a letter

to Emma. She knew Emma would have lots of questions, but since she didn't yet have the answers, she'd just tell her what she did know and write again once she was settled in Miradero.

Dear Emma,

This is the hardest letter I've ever written, and I really wish I could have told you this in person. I can't come to your birthday party. Grandpa is sending my dad out West, to a little town called Miradero. Dad's going to oversee a new rail line that will go all the way to the ocean. Dad says it's a very important project, and that if it's not successful, JP & Sons will lose everything. So Dad has to go. And that means he's going to be living out there.

Here's the harder part. I'm going with him. Grandpa and Aunt Cora want me to stay in the city, but how can I do that? I've already lost my mom. I don't want to live without my dad, too. So I'm leaving.

This morning. That's why there's no time to say good-bye in person.

I don't know how long we'll be gone. Dad says it could be a long time.

I know we always talk about new adventures, but this one is happening so fast, I'm scared. And even though I'm not yet on the train, I already miss you!

Emma, I hope with all my heart that you have the best birthday party ever. And I promise that I will write you lots of letters. As soon as I can, I will come back for a visit. And as soon as you can, you must come and visit me.

I will send you my address when I find out what it is.

Your best friend forever and ever,

Lucky

PS: Don't let Madame Barrow turn you into a work of art. I like you just the way you are.

PPS: I hope you like the present I got for you.

When Jim headed downstairs, he found Lucky sitting on her stack of trunks in front of the door. "You're ready?" he asked with surprise.

She nodded, trying to present him with a cheerful face, but her stomach still ached. It had been odd not to put on her school uniform. But almost everything about this morning was odd. Jim knelt beside her and took her hand in both of his. For as long as she could remember, her father's gaze had calmed her. When the world felt too loud or too judgmental, she'd look into his blue eyes and feel safe. "It's perfectly normal to be afraid," he said. "But not everything ahead of us is unknown. We'll be together. We'll have a nice house. You'll make new friends."

"An I hope ya find a nice housekeeper," said Mrs. MacFinn as she dried her hands on a tea towel. Lucky noticed that her nose and eyes were equally puffy and red. "Ya need ta be fed."

"Of course we could never replace you," Jim told her with a wink. "No one can make a chicken liver pie like Mrs. MacFinn."

"Aye, that be tha truth."

Jim turned back to Lucky. "Miradero will have everything we need, like a general store and...well, I *think* there's a general store. Actually, I'm not sure." He shrugged. "I guess we'll figure it out when we get there."

Mrs. MacFinn began crying again. "I cannae believe ya be leavin'."

"Now, now." Jim stood and patted her on the back. "You and your husband will be happy here. This is your house, too, and with Mr. MacFinn's help, you'll look after it for us. Lucky and I are relying on you to keep the place clean and tidy. And one day, we'll be back." Mrs. MacFinn blew her nose loudly into a handkerchief.

The familiar clip-clop of horse hooves drew Lucky's attention. She looked out the window just as a white mare and carriage stopped in front of the house. The driver jumped down, opened the carriage door, and James Prescott Sr. emerged. He set his top hat upon his head and pursed his lips in a sour expression. Then he shook his fist at his driver and began hollering about something. "Looks like he's crankier than usual," Jim said. "Defensive positions, everyone." Lucky laughed for the first time that morning.

Jim opened the door, greeting his father with exaggerated surprise. "Father? What brings you here on this lovely spring morning?"

"You know dang well what brings me here!" James Sr. bellowed. "I just got your note!" He stomped into the foyer, then scowled at Lucky. "I'm not happy about this, young lady. You're going against my wishes."

He was *definitely* crankier than usual. "Grandpa, I—"

Jim stepped protectively in front of Lucky. "Father, I don't mean to seem disrespectful, but if I'm going to Miradero, then Lucky's going to Miradero. I'm her father and she's my daughter. We're a team and we're staying together."

James Sr. folded his arms, his scowl deepening. "Is this what you want as well, Lucky?"

Lucky peered around her father's waist and nodded.

"Is this your final decision?" Lucky nodded again. James Sr. exhaled so violently, his mustache vibrated. "I declare, you two are the most stubborn people I have ever met!"

"We get that from you, Father." Jim patted his dad on the back.

"Very well. So be it!" As those words echoed off the foyer walls, James Sr.'s expression relaxed and his anger was replaced with resignation. Lucky couldn't remember ever seeing her grandfather defeated. "Just remember, young lady, if you change your mind and decide you don't like it out there, your aunt and I will welcome you back with open arms."

"Thank you." Lucky hurried forward and hugged her grandfather around his large belly. She loved him dearly. It was true what Mrs. MacFinn always said about him— that his bark was worse than his bite. The hug lasted only a moment because she realized someone was missing. "Where's Aunt Cora?"

"No idea whatsoever. She read your father's note that you two were leaving this morning, and she disappeared. I assume she's at one of her blasted meetings. Don't know why she spends so much time with all those committees. Seems to me we've got enough culture in this city already."

Lucky frowned. She'd wanted to give her aunt a good-bye hug. As much as Cora was way too strict for her liking, as Lucky had heard her dad refer to her aunt, Lucky knew she was going to miss her. Were those meetings really more important to her? "Would you say good-bye for me?" Lucky asked.

"Of course I will." Was that a tear in her grandfather's eye? He quickly turned away.

Jim left instructions with Mr. MacFinn to deliver a letter to Madame Barrow, explaining Lucky's withdrawal from school. Lucky gave him her letter for Emma and the birthday present she'd picked out and wrapped weeks ago. It was a leather-bound journal in which Emma could write her own stories. Mr. MacFinn promised to make the deliveries that very day.

The driver placed all the trunks atop the carriage and secured them with a rope. Then James Sr., Jim, and Lucky climbed in. Mr. and Mrs. MacFinn stood on the porch, waving. It was the most tearful morning Lucky could remember, and she was glad when she could no longer see the old couple. She was having trouble holding back her own tears!

The journey to the station was uneventful. No carriage accidents blocked the road. No cowgirls or show horses drew crowds. The roadway remained clear. "When we get there, I'll have them attach the Prescott car," James Sr. said. Like most families of wealth and influence, the Prescotts possessed a private railcar that could be coupled to any train, for traveling in comfort and privacy. And as the owner of the railroad, James Sr. had the fanciest car ever built, complete with a living room, sleeping room, kitchen, and an office for business.

"Father, that's not necessary," Jim said. "In fact, I think it's best we don't arrive in Miradero like a king and his princess. I don't want to make that first impression."

James Sr. grumbled beneath his mustache. Then he pounded a clenched fist on the side of the carriage. "I'll not have my family traveling in one of the passenger cars with the riffraff. If you won't use our private car, then you'll take a first-class cabin, and you'll not argue with me on this one!"

Jim nodded at Lucky and she nodded back. They knew when to pick their battles.

Lucky had been to the train station many times in her life, but never with so much luggage. She'd taken day trips to visit her cousins, but this particular journey would take many days and require sleeping on the train, which she'd never done. These unknowns, coupled with the fact that she would be cooped up, heightened her feelings of trepidation. Once they closed the doors, would she feel like a caged bird? Her legs twitched just thinking about it.

A porter stacked the trunks onto a wheeled cart and took them away to load them onboard the train. The station was loud, with attendants hollering directions and vendors hawking wares. Passengers rushed about. There were families with kids in tow. Couples arm in arm. One lady carried a cat in a wooden box. The poor thing looked out from the box with wide eyes, appearing as scared as Lucky secretly felt. Where was everyone going?

The air was stifling and thick with steam and the overpowering scent of hot grease. This was James Sr.'s world, his kingdom, and he appeared years younger as he walked proudly past his workers, tipping his top hat now and then. Lucky and Jim followed, making their way through the station house and out onto the platform. A train waited on the tracks. The initials *JP* were painted on the sides in gold leaf. The engine was fired and ready to go, hissing and gurgling, making quick *pshhht* sounds. The driver leaned out and saluted James Sr. "Top of the morning to ya, sir," he shouted. James Sr. saluted back. They passed the crowded passenger cars, where people reached out windows to wave good-bye to friends and family. They passed a luggage car and a mail car.

"All aboard!" the conductor called as he paced back and forth. When he recognized James Sr., he hurried over. "Good morning, sir; are you traveling today? I had no idea. Shall we send for your private car?"

"My son and granddaughter are traveling to Miradero, and they will require only a first-class cabin," James Sr. said.

The conductor raised his eyebrows, but wisely didn't question this decision. "Right this way."

The first-class car was at the back of the train, the optimal location because it was far from the hot and noisy engine. As they reached it, James Sr. stopped walking and set a hand on his son's shoulder. "Jim," he said. "I'm an old man. You know what that means?"

"That you're wiser than me?" Jim responded with a wry smile.

"Yes, obviously. But it also means that I'm not sure how much time I have left." Was that another tear in his eye? "I expect you to bring Lucky back for a visit sooner rather than later. Do you understand? I intend to see my granddaughter many more times before I'm called home."

Jim pushed his blond hair away from his eyes, his expression one of sudden pain. "Yes, of course, Father. Don't worry. You'll see Lucky again. I promise." Then he gave his father a bear hug. "I love you."

"I love you, too, Son."

"Last call. All aboard!" the conductor hollered.

Lucky hugged her grandfather again. Her heart pounded as she climbed the steps to the first-class car. This was it. Not a story by Jules Verne. Not a dream. They were really leaving for an adventure. But just as she reached the top step, a voice yelled, "Wait for me!" Lucky turned and gasped.

Cora Prescott was running—*in public*. With pure determination frozen on her face, she frantically pumped her legs, purse in one hand, her other hand holding her hat in place. Lucky grinned and jumped back onto the platform. "Aunt Cora!" she called. Her aunt had come to say good-bye after all. But that's when she noticed a porter running alongside Cora, his wheeled cart stacked with trunks. Each trunk was embossed with the gold initials *CP*.

"Cora, what is the meaning of this?" James Sr. asked.

She came to an abrupt stop, gasping for breath. "Father, you cannot deter me."

"Ma'am, the train is scheduled to leave promptly," the conductor told her.

"Then I suggest you get my trunks onboard quickly." The porter began to lug them onto the first-class luggage car.

"Cora?" James Sr. bellowed.

"Father!" She stomped her foot. "There's no time to debate."

"Wait." Lucky's joy at seeing her aunt vanished in a heartbeat. "Are you coming *with* us?" Maybe her aunt was taking a trip to a different town. Any town. *But please, oh please, not to Miradero.*

"Yes indeed, I am coming with you," she replied with stiff resolve. The pheasant feather on her hat bobbed in agreement. "Cora Prescott is going to Miradero."

Everyone looked at James Sr. Lucky clenched her jaw. Her grandfather appeared unable to speak. His mouth hung open in shock.

Cora raised a hand in the air, as if giving a speech to her Social Betterment Society. Even though strands of her bun had come undone and her hat was askew, she still held herself with confidence. "I searched my heart and my conscience, and I believe, without a doubt, that there is no way I can allow Lucky to be on her own in that wild place. She has no mother and thus it is my duty, as her closest female relative, to look after her."

"Cora, this is unnecessary," Jim said. "Lucky and I will be fine. Besides, how can you leave your clubs and committees?"

"My mind is set. I am determined to look after Lucky and bring civility to the frontier. A challenge has been presented to me, and Prescotts do not run from challenges."

Lucky cringed. Aunt Cora was truly coming with them? This was terrible. Now the West would be filled with rules. There'd be appearances to keep up, and all those lectures. But there was still a chance this wouldn't happen. She looked to her grandfather, hoping he'd forbid it.

Instead, what came out of his mouth surprised

everyone, even the conductor. "I think it sounds like an excellent idea."

What? Lucky couldn't believe it. He was letting Cora go to Miradero? She looked closer at her grandfather's face and detected a slight smile hiding beneath his mustache. Was he secretly glad to have Cora leaving? Of course he was. She probably lectured him all the time, too. Now he'd be able to chew with his mouth open, to eat with whichever fork he wanted. He'd be able to enjoy a meal in peace.

The train whistle blew. "Last call! All aboard!"

"We'd better hurry," Jim said. He hustled Lucky and Cora up the steps. As the train began to pull out of the station, Lucky turned to wave good-bye to her grandfather, but steam swirled around him, erasing him from view. Lucky told herself that she'd see him again. That she'd see Emma again, too.

A porter led them into their first-class cabin. Two bench seats faced each other, comfortably padded and elegantly upholstered. Purple velvet curtains with pretty yellow sashes hung on the window, and a lovely Persian rug decorated the floor. There was a small closet with a shelf for small personal items. Lucky pressed her face to the window, watching as the station slowly disappeared. Cora collapsed onto the seat across from her. "Cora? Are you okay?" Jim asked.

She didn't reply. She stared straight ahead, wide-eyed and pale. Lucky had never known her aunt to be speechless.

"Ma'am, would you like some coffee?" The first-class car came with an attendant, who began to pour black coffee into a china cup. "How far are you going?" he asked Jim.

"All the way to Miradero." Jim handed the cup to Cora, who took it with trembling hands.

"Miradero?" the attendant said. "That's sure a long way to go. Why, that's the end of the line."

"End of the line?" Cora gasped. "Oh dear, what have I done?"

10

Lucky, Jim, and Cora spent two nights in their private sleeping berths—snug bunks that were tucked behind curtains. Lucky's bunk was warm and cozy, and despite all the questions and worries swirling around in her head, the thrumming of the wheels against the tracks quickly lulled her to sleep. When she awoke on the third morning, the first thing she did was roll over and look out the window. "Wow."

The landscape had changed dramatically. Gone were the cities. Gone was the river they'd been following. The train now chugged its way through a mountain pass. Craggy gray mountains loomed overhead, some still wearing the last vestiges of snow on their peaks, like hats. The sight was beautiful.

Lucky got dressed and slid out of the bunk. Jim was awake, drinking his coffee and reading a paper from the day before. "When will we get there?" Lucky asked.

"We should arrive tomorrow, midday," he said. Then he put a finger to his lip. "Your aunt is still sleeping. Let's not wake her unnecessarily."

Lucky agreed. They'd spent most of yesterday listening to Cora complain. The train was too bumpy.

The air was too stuffy. Jim had politely reminded her that she could get off at any station and take a return train home. "Prescotts do not run from challenges," she'd replied.

As they drew closer to their new home, more questions popped into Lucky's head. She wanted to know everything. "Dad, where will we live when we get to Miradero?"

"Your grandfather hired workers to build a house out there, a couple of years back. He knew he'd need a place to stay when the expansion of the railroad got started."

"What kind of house?"

"I've never seen it, but knowing your grandfather, it won't be a one-room cabin." Jim chuckled. Then he noticed Lucky's swinging legs. "Let's get some exercise," he said. They walked up and down the corridor as quickly as they could, then turned it into a race to see who could walk the fastest. Five times up and down. Then five more. Each challenge ended in a tie. Cora would not have approved, but she was still sleeping. Lucky and her father raced until they were both out of breath. The exercise helped settle Lucky's worried thoughts. But with so much unknown waiting for her at the end of the line, the relief was temporary.

It was unusual for Cora to sleep in, but she wasn't

used to train travel and had been feeling out of sorts. By mid-morning she appeared, dressed in a high-necked blouse with a string of pearls and matching pearl earrings. Her hair was arranged in its usual tidy bun, but the look on her face was anything but usual. "Oh dear," she said, placing a hand over her stomach. "I'm a bit… unsettled."

"Maybe you need some fresh air," Jim suggested.

"It is my professional opinion that you are suffering from motion sickness," a man said. Jim had struck up a conversation with two passengers from another first-class cabin and invited them back for coffee and cake. This fellow's name was Dr. Merriweather. He stood not much taller than Lucky, was rather thin, and his round eyes reminded her of the cod Mrs. MacFinn often brought back from the fishmonger's store. The other guest was the opposite of Dr. Merriweather—grand in size, with legs that stretched out so far, they kept tripping the attendant. His name was Mr. Bart and he owned a cattle ranch.

Mr. Bart took a long drink of coffee. "Nothing to be ashamed of, ma'am. Even a big fellow like me can get train sick." He propped the china cup on his belly. The cup looked ridiculously small compared to the fellow's large hands.

Lucky felt sorry for her aunt. But she was also happy that she wasn't suffering from motion sickness. She'd hate to miss out on the cake. Of course it couldn't be as good as the cake Emma was serving at her birthday today. Lucky hesitated mid-bite. She imagined that Emma would be getting ready, putting on her party dress, helping to decorate the house. Lucky was supposed to get there early and help, too. Then they'd wait together at the front window, watching as the carriages pulled up and the guests arrived. Lucky would sit beside Emma while the presents were opened, keeping a list of names so Emma could write thank-you cards. Lucky and Emma would partner up for all the games, as usual. She sighed. *Happy birthday, Emma,* she thought. Her thoughts were interrupted when Dr. Merriweather cleared his throat.

"Allow me to ease your suffering," he told Cora. "I have a special tonic, brewed for this kind of situation." He reached into a black leather satchel and pulled out a corked bottle. Lucky happened to be sitting closest, so he handed the bottle to her.

She read the label out loud. "Dr. Merriweather's Homebrewed Tummy Tonic, guaranteed to relieve symptoms of digestive assault, including dizziness, discombobulation, nausea, gaseous outbursts—"

"Lucky!" Cora interrupted.

"That's what it says." Lucky handed the bottle over to Cora.

Cora inspected the label, then narrowed her eyes. "Dr. Merriweather, where, exactly, did you get your medical degree?"

Dr. Merriweather cleared his throat. "My degree, my dear Miss Prescott, is not of the *medical* variety. I am a doctor of *philosophical matters* and a maker of tonics. Which I sell. That particular bottle is available for purchase."

"No, thank you." Cora handed the bottle back to Lucky, who returned it to the doctor. "I have no need of any homemade tonic. I will wait until we get to Miradero, where I shall consult with a *medical* doctor." She frowned and, once again, placed a hand over her stomach.

"As you wish." He blinked his bulbous eyes, then tucked the tonic back into his bag. "But you never know if you'll find a doctor out West. And you do seem discombobulated."

"I am *discombobulated*, dear sir, because I am going to a godforsaken place where there may or may not be a doctor."

"Calm down, Cora. I'm sure we'll find a doctor in

Miradero." Jim tried to change the subject. "Isn't this cake delicious? Would either of you like another piece?"

"Don't mind if I do," Mr. Bart said, turning two slices into a single hefty serving.

Dr. Merriweather politely declined. But he continued to talk to Cora. "I have other tonics that might be of interest to you. For the various troubles that can arise in the Wild West."

Now this was getting interesting. "What kind of troubles?" Lucky asked.

"I had a customer—out in Porter, bless her soul." He ran his fingers along his thin mustache, smoothing the edges. "She was minding her business putting on her boots one morning and was overcome by a terrible sharp pain. When she turned the boot over, guess what fell right out?"

Cora's hand flew to her heart. Lucky sat up straight. "What?"

"A rattlesnake. They hide in the most inconvenient places." He pulled out another corked bottle. "However, if she'd possessed Dr. Merriweather's Vitality Tonic, she might be alive today. It vitalizes the nervous system. And also removes stains." He smiled, revealing a gold tooth.

"Those rattlers are a dang nuisance," Mr. Bart confirmed.

"Well, that's a good lesson for us to remember," Jim said. "Always check our shoes in the morning."

Cora ignored the bottle, so Dr. Merriweather returned it to his bag and grabbed another. "There was a gentleman last month, minding his own business out in Dunlop, just sitting on a rock enjoying his lunch when, well, you can guess."

"He got bit by a rattlesnake?" Lucky asked.

"Worse. He was attacked by a scorpion. If he'd taken Dr. Merriweather's Daily Healthful Tonic he might have survived. But instead, he keeled over, right on the spot."

"I daresay that's enough," Cora said.

"It also smoothes wrinkles and fades freckles," added Dr. Merriweather.

"Ain't just the critters you've got to worry about." Mr. Bart wiped chocolate cake from his face, then pushed back his cowboy hat as if he had really important news to deliver. "There's dangerous folk out there, too. Got cattle rustlers and bank robbers. Why, a train was robbed just last week. Bandits came onboard and took everyone's jewelry and money."

Jim nodded with concern. "Train robberies are on the rise, unfortunately. JP & Sons has issued wanted posters up and down the line, but we haven't caught them yet."

Lucky imagined their train being robbed. She'd have her first adventure to write about. What a letter that would make for Emma.

"They haven't been caught 'cause there ain't enough sheriffs to go round," Mr. Bart said. "Some of the newer towns got no lawkeepers at all."

"No police?" Cora began fanning herself with a silk fan. She looked near to fainting.

"Ma'am, are you suffering from the vapors?" Dr. Merriweather asked. "I've got a—"

"She's fine," Jim assured him. "Cora, let's not get all worked up before we get to Miradero."

"How come you folks are going to Miradero?" asked Mr. Bart.

"I'm going to oversee the extension of the railroad from Miradero to the Pacific," Jim explained.

"You don't say. Sounds like a big job. And what about you, little lady?"

"I'll be going to school," Lucky replied happily. "Have you ever been to Miradero? Do you know what the school is like?"

Cora stopped fanning. "Indeed, I have been wondering the same thing. Is the private school for boys only? I hear that is often the case in small towns, but I'm hopeful they will make an exception and allow girls to attend classes."

"Private school?" Mr. Bart looked puzzled, as if they'd just asked him what road led to the moon. "There ain't no private school, ma'am. Last time I was in Miradero there was a schoolhouse at the end of town, just past the blacksmith shop. There's one teacher for all the kids."

"One teacher?" Lucky asked. At Madame Barrow's she'd had a math teacher, a language teacher, *and* a history teacher.

"There's no need for more than one teacher, on account there's just one room in the schoolhouse."

"One room?" Cora's fan dropped to the carpet. "How can you possibly give children a proper education in *one room*? Where do they study music? Where do they practice art? What about a school library?"

Lucky tried to imagine one room with everyone crammed into it. She began to imagine the kids, too. What did they look like? What did they wear? How different would she be? Would she fit in?

"One room is unacceptable," Cora declared.

Once again, Jim tried to keep his sister from blowing things out of proportion. "Cora, we can't know the answers to these things until we get there." He returned the fan to her.

Cora beat the air with renewed vigor. "If the school is not up to our standards, then I will take over teaching Lucky."

Lucky cringed. Cora as her teacher? This was terrible news. How could Lucky possibly make new friends if she was stuck at home with her aunt all day?

How difficult would it be to find a rattlesnake, capture it, and stick it into Cora's boot? Lucky wondered. Of course, she didn't want the snake to bite her aunt, just scare her enough to go back home and leave Lucky and her dad in peace!

11

First came the chugging of an engine in the distance and the vibration of wheels against tracks. Then a long trail of smoke appeared, twisting in the air like a snake. The stallion stood, his hooves firmly planted, waiting with anticipation. His cousins gathered around him, their gazes fixed on the horizon.

And then it appeared, the black creature that carried people to this place. Long and sleek, it moved toward the herd. Closer and closer, louder and louder. The stallion snorted and stomped his hoof. He playfully tossed his head. Then he called to the younger horses, the ones like him who wanted to run. It was a game they were fond of, a race to see who could gallop the fastest. The older horses shook their heads, for they knew the dangers that could arise if one broke away from the safety of the herd. They snorted. The stallion ignored them. He was stubborn, a trait that came in handy during winter searches for food when he refused to give up.

But being stubborn can also lead to trouble.

The stallion's sister butted him with her forehead,

trying to move his attention to other things. But at that moment he wasn't thinking about anything except the chase. He stepped away from her, his willful nature fixated on one thing—to prove himself the fastest.

He would wait for the rolling beast to come closer.

12

They spent a third night on the train, and the following morning the first stop was the town of Winslow, where most of the passengers disembarked—among them Dr. Merriweather and Mr. Bart. Though small, Winslow was considered a bustling metropolis in this part of the world, and it was the last stop before the train headed into the high desert. Since very few passengers went all the way to the end of the line, most of the passenger cars were replaced with cars carrying livestock and supplies. Lucky was allowed to get off the train with her father. "Don't get your dress dirty!" Cora called after her.

What a relief to be outside. While Jim bought a local newspaper, Lucky stretched her legs. She played chase with a boy and his dog. She bought a bag of peppermint candy. She explored every nook she could find. There was a barbershop where a man wearing a golden badge was getting his beard trimmed. *A real sheriff*, Lucky realized. There was a hat shop that sold mostly cowboy hats. She tried one on but it was much too big. She watched while a man ushered some enormous pigs up a ramp into one of the livestock cars. She peered inside a crate that was full of fluffy golden chicks. And everywhere she looked, she saw cowboys, with their leather britches and colorful bandanas. *I'm really here. In the Wild West.*

"Lucky," her father called, waving her over. "You've got to try these. They're tortillas." Just outside the train station, a woman sat beside a small fire, rolling dough and frying it in butter. Jim handed a tortilla to Lucky. It was golden and warm. She held it in her hand and took a bite.

"Delicious," she said. She ate two more. Good thing Cora couldn't see her eating without utensils. What a scene that would be!

"Lucky, do you remember why this town is so special?" her father asked.

"Of course I remember. It's where you met Mom."

He nodded, then pointed. "The circus tent was set up right over there."

Images filled Lucky's mind as Jim's story came to life at the end of the street. He and his fellow ranch hands waiting in line to see the circus. The monkey who collected their tickets. Her mother riding around the ring on horseback. Without this town, Lucky might not have been born. She smiled and finished her tortilla. "I like it here," she said. "Will Miradero be this nice?" But she knew her father didn't have the answer.

The train whistle blew and they made their way back to their cabin. Lucky passed the time by finishing *Journey to the Center of the Earth*, but then she had nothing to do. She didn't know how she'd endure another long morning stuck in there. Cora's motion sickness seemed to be wearing off, but that meant she was more talkative. Cora's stories weren't about scorpion attacks or bank robberies. Rather, she talked about a Russian art exhibit one of her committees had organized for a museum. "We should all be exposed to great works of art," Cora said. "Art enlivens the soul. I'm sure Miradero doesn't have an art museum with majestic paintings like these. They probably go only to rodeos or to the circus."

"Cora," Jim said.

Cora looked at Lucky with sincere regret. "Oh, dear, I didn't mean that as an insult." Her eyebrows furrowed. "I'm sure your mother's circus was the loveliest show. But you understand, don't you, when I say the circus isn't art? It's *entertainment*."

"*El Circo Dos Grillos* was an amazing circus," Jim said. "I wish you could have seen it, Cora; you'd change your mind. What I witnessed was truly art." Lucky wished she could have seen her mother's performance. Even though her father's stories were vivid, nothing could beat actually being in the audience.

What a thrill it would have been to watch her mother dance with the horses. "Milagro wasn't only a master at handling the horses; she earned their trust," Jim continued. "Their full trust, as if she were one of them. As if she were part horse."

"I've never heard anything so ridiculous," Cora said. "A person is a person and a horse is a horse. Horse riding is dangerous. Those animals are powerful beasts and cannot be trusted. You never know when they might toss you right off their backs."

Lucky didn't feel like arguing with Cora. She could deal with not riding horses, but what she couldn't deal with was all this sitting. Sitting and sitting. She desperately wanted to get off the train again. To run! To see her new home. To explore her new neighborhood. This was becoming worse than recitations. That familiar twitchy feeling crept into her legs. She stretched them out, accidentally kicking Cora. "Sorry."

"We're almost there," her father told her. "Soon. Very, very soon."

Very soon wasn't soon enough. Lucky could barely contain the excitement that was building. She felt like a teakettle about to whistle.

While Cora yammered on and on about the importance of art, Lucky grabbed her drawing supplies and tried sketching. She scribbled some patterns, swirls, flowers, and hearts; then she drew a birthday cake. Jim sat across from her, watching while she added little rosettes to the icing. "Hey, sweet pea, missing your friends already?"

"Yesterday was Emma's birthday. I bet they had so much fun."

"But we're doing something even better; we're having an adventure." Jim leaned forward and nudged her, but it was hard for Lucky to muster a grin. Sure, the adventure had begun, but thus far they'd been stuck on a train. And to make matters worse, there was nothing interesting to look at anymore. Gone were the cities and towns. Gone were the grand forests and snowcapped mountains. Sometimes they'd pass a pile of equipment left behind by railroad workers, or the occasional abandoned wagon wheel. But mostly there was an endless expanse of land. Lots and lots of land. When would Miradero appear?

Lucky pushed her drawing pad aside and rested her arms and chin on the window ledge. She pressed her face to the window. "How come those mountains look weird?"

"They're called *mesas*," Jim explained. "*Mesa* means 'table' in Spanish. Think of them as tabletop mountains, because they have those flat tops."

"How come they're red?" Lucky asked.

"The color is from iron oxide. Wait till you see them when the setting sun hits them. It's quite a sight." Jim's face took on a dreamy look. Was he remembering a moment he'd spent with Lucky's mother?

A shrill sound startled Lucky and Jim from their thoughts. "The train whistle," Lucky said. "We must be passing by something exciting. Can I go out and see?"

Jim shrugged. "Sure."

"Certainly not," Cora said. "It's dangerous out there. A train is no place for a young lady to go gallivanting about."

"We aren't in the city anymore, Cora. Maybe it's time to give Lucky a little more freedom." And thus began an argument Lucky had heard way too many times in her life—her aunt taking the protective stance, trying to keep Lucky from getting hurt; her father pointing out that they couldn't protect Lucky from *everything*. All those times Lucky had asked to ride a bike, or asked to ride a horse, Cora had always won the argument because somehow Cora always knew someone who'd gotten hurt in that very activity.

"My friend Lucy's cousin's husband's employer fell off a train and was never seen again!" Cora told Jim. "And you're going to allow your daughter to go out there?"

The whistle blew again, and what it said to Lucky was, *Hey, get out here, you're missing something!*

Lucky didn't wait for the argument's outcome. While Cora and Jim battled, she made her getaway, hurrying out of the first-class car and into a car filled with luggage. Moving as quickly as she could, she passed her own trunks and Cora's, with the initials *CP*. Why had the whistle blown? Was there something too close to the tracks? Like a wild animal?

Or train robbers?

During the stopover in Winslow, where cargo cars had been added, a caboose had been added as well. Lucky opened the door and found herself in the conductor's office, complete with a desk, a bunk, and a sink. The conductor wasn't there. Surely he wouldn't mind if Lucky took a peek outside. She hurried through, then flung open the back door. Fresh air greeted her as she stepped onto the caboose's balcony.

Lucky gasped. Now that she stood in the open air, the train seemed to be moving faster. The sensation caught her off guard and she stumbled, grabbing the rail for balance. The tracks behind stretched like two lines in a sketchbook, all the way to the horizon. On either side lay open prairie, basking beneath an endless blue sky. Lucky smiled and lifted her face. What a great feeling, to glide along, the wind on her skin. She wished the train could go faster!

Movement caught the corner of her eye. She darted to the right side of the caboose and gripped the railing. The mystery of the train whistle was solved.

A herd of horses!

Dozens of them galloped alongside the train, their hooves thundering. They varied in color—some were solid black, a few were black with white faces, others were chocolate with white spots. But it was a stallion who caught Lucky's attention. His coat was tan, like the color of dried grass, with a black mane, black tail, and black legs. He pulled away from the herd, managing to keep pace with the train. How could a horse run so fast? Lucky shivered with excitement. He was the most beautiful horse she'd ever seen. He galloped closer until he was parallel to her. He turned his head, as curious about her as she was about him. She noticed a white stripe from his forehead to his muzzle. Without considering the danger, without any sense of fear, Lucky leaned over the railing and reached out her hand. Their eyes locked. If she leaned a bit farther, she might be able to touch him. Oh, how desperately she wanted to touch him. But his gaze darted away, and that's when they both noticed something.

"Look out!" Lucky cried.

The stallion veered away just in time, as a rope

flew through the air, barely missing his neck. Two men on horseback appeared out of nowhere. They swung ropes over their heads. "Get him!" one of them shouted. The rest of the herd broke away and headed toward the distant hills, but the men didn't follow. They were focused on the stallion.

Why were they trying to catch him? "Leave him alone!" Lucky screamed. The stallion kept galloping, the men in close pursuit. The ropes swung again; this time one reached its target, looping around the stallion's neck. The man pulled the rope taut, slowing the beautiful horse just enough for the other man to loop a second rope around his neck. As the stallion reared and bucked, a desperate whinny filled the air, but he couldn't break free. "No!" Lucky cried. A pair of hands grabbed her and pulled her away from the railing. "Leave me alone!"

"Fortuna Esperanza Navarro Prescott!" Her aunt's angry voice boomed in her ear. "You get back inside this minute!" With surprising strength, Cora pulled Lucky into the caboose's cabin. Lucky caught one last look at the stallion, who stood alongside the tracks, straining against the ropes. Then the whole scene disappeared into the horizon.

"You are incorrigible," Cora said, wagging a finger. "Return to your father this instant."

Lucky didn't hear a word her aunt said. She could think about only one thing. With a swift turn on her heels, she raced back to their cabin. "Dad!" she called as she fell onto the seat next to him.

"What's going on?" he asked. Their cabin was on the opposite side of the train, so he'd missed the whole thing.

"Dad, I—"

"Outrageous, that's what it was, flinging herself at the rails," Cora reported. Strands of her hair had come loose in the wind, so she began to tuck them into place. "With no regard to safety. She would have jumped right off the back of the train if I hadn't stopped her."

Jim lowered his newspaper. "Jumped off? What are you talking about?"

Lucky pushed out the words as fast as she could. "I wanted to help him."

"Help who? What happened?"

She had her father's full attention now, and she needed to be quick before Cora interrupted again. She strung her sentences together in one long, breathless explanation. "There was this horse, this beautiful horse, and he was running next to the train and he looked right at me, and all I wanted to do was touch him so I reached out my hand and I think he was going to let me pet him, but these horrible men threw ropes on him!"

Jim set his hand on her knee. "Lucky, take a breath. You're turning blue."

"Dad, it was terrible! Why did they throw ropes around him?"

Jim nodded as he began to understand what Lucky had witnessed. "Well, those men are called *mesteñeros*. They catch mustangs."

"Mustangs?"

"Mustangs are the wild horses that live in these parts. Often they'll round up the entire herd, then funnel them into a pen. But the really skilled riders will use ropes, like you saw. After the *mesteñeros* capture a mustang, they take him back to a ranch to be broken."

"Broken? That's terrible. Why would they do something like that? They're such pretty horses."

"Oh, Lucky, *broken* is a term that means 'trained.' They slowly take the wildness out of the mustangs and tame them, so they can be ridden. They won't hurt the horse you saw." But Lucky wasn't convinced. It didn't sound fair, to take such a lovely wild creature away from his family. Jim reached forward and pulled her into a hug. "He'll be fine. I promise."

With hands on hips, Cora shook her head in disbelief. "Why are you hugging her? I'm not done yelling. Didn't you hear me? She nearly fell off the train."

"I *didn't* almost fall," Lucky insisted. In truth, maybe she had reached out too far. But in that moment she'd felt mesmerized, the eyes of the horse meeting hers. She'd felt drawn to him.

"It seems to me that a beast like that should stay in the wild," Cora said.

Lucky completely agreed. And then the sound she'd been waiting for filled her ears.

"Last stop, Miradero. Everyone must disembark! Last stop, Miradero!"

13

Wheels screeched against track as the train slowed.

Finally!

Lucky was off the train before Cora could stop her. After a cacophony of spluttering and hissing noises, the great steam engine fell silent. Her ears hummed a bit from the long trip but it didn't bother her. They'd arrived!

With a brisk, excited pace, Lucky walked along the platform. She passed men unloading crates labeled DYNAMITE. Cattle mooed and bellowed from inside their cars, giving off a powerful scent. Or was that from the pigs in the next car over? A painted sign hung above the platform. WELCOME TO MIRADERO. She hurried into the station house, a small room with only one bench seat and a ticket window where an old man snored, his head resting on the counter. An orange cat perched next to him, watching the way cats do—curious yet uninterested at the same time. The station house walls were covered in wanted posters. WANTED FOR TRAIN ROBBERY. WANTED FOR CATTLE RUSTLING. Lucky's eyes widened with excitement. WANTED FOR BANK ROBBERY. This place was wild! Cora was going to squeal when she read these.

The train schedule was posted on a large board, as

was an advertisement for *Dr. Merriweather's Snake Oil Tonic*, but Lucky wasn't interested in any of those things. She desperately wanted to see where she was going to spend the next months, maybe years, of her life. Two doors stood ahead of her, each with a window glowing with sunshine. What would she find on the other side? Would the streets be teeming with cowboys? Would bandits be roaming in gangs? Would Miradero be as untamed as Cora feared?

That would be amazing!

Lucky pushed open the doors and stepped into…

…stifling midday heat.

The noon sun hovered directly overhead. Lucky loosened the green sash on her dress. Talk about being way overdressed. Some of her layers needed to come off, and soon. And it was so bright!

Jim and Cora joined Lucky outside the station. "Smell that country air!" Jim said, expanding his lungs with enthusiasm.

"It smells like manure," Cora complained, wrinkling her nose.

Jim laughed. "You'll get used to the odor."

As Lucky's eyes adjusted to the sun, she took a long, sweeping look at her new surroundings. They'd arrived in a green valley surrounded by tabletop mountains.

Dozens of juniper trees grew next to the station. Lucky had seen junipers before, but these were tall, with wild, twisted branches, not neatly trimmed into hedges like the ones in the city. Large boulders dotted the landscape, with yellow flowers peeking between. A dirt road led away from the station to some buildings in the distance. "That must be the edge of town," Jim said.

"Are we walking there?" Lucky asked. "It's not that far from here."

"I certainly hope we're not walking in this heat." Cora fiddled with her tight collar. "My goodness, is it always this hot?"

"You'll get used to that, too," Jim told her.

A man approached. He wore a plaid shirt with the sleeves rolled up. A wide-brimmed hat shaded his face. He tipped his hat at Cora. "Hello, folks, you must be the Prescotts. I'm John Mercer. I do the bookkeeping for JP & Sons." He extended his hand and he and Jim shook. Jim introduced him to Cora and Lucky. "Looks like you made it in one piece. How was your trip?"

"It took forever," Lucky complained.

John pushed his thick glasses up his nose. "Imagine how long it took in the old days when you had to come by wagon train." He pointed behind them. "I brought the company wagon. We'll load up your luggage, and

I'll drive you to your house. It'll be nice having a family living up there. Been vacant since Mr. Prescott Sr. had it built." A station worker helped wheel the trunks to the wagon, then Jim and John loaded them. Sweat beaded on Jim's forehead. His wool jacket and waistcoat were proving too much in the sun. "You won't be needing formal clothes, Mr. Prescott," John told him. "It's casual clothing hereabouts."

"Good to know," Jim said as he stripped off his jacket and flung it into the wagon. Then he, too, rolled up his sleeves. Cora pursed her lips but said nothing.

Once the trunks were loaded, Jim helped Cora into the wagon. She and Lucky took the back bench while Jim sat up front next to John. Cora opened her parasol, creating shade for herself and Lucky. John and Jim began discussing railroad issues. Jim wanted to stop at the JP & Sons office to introduce himself to the staff. Lucky wasn't much interested in what they were talking about. She was watching the two brown horses pulling the wagon. "Are those mustangs?" she asked.

"Nope. If you want mustangs, you'll need to go to Al Granger's place."

Lucky scooted forward and leaned between John and her father. "Does that mean Mr. Granger takes them from the wild?"

"Al specializes in breaking wild horses. He's the best horse wrangler in these parts. I'm surprised you know about mustangs, being from the city and all."

Lucky didn't really know anything about mustangs, but unlike the stallion, these two horses weren't fighting against the reins. They seemed perfectly happy. *Could a wild mustang be equally happy pulling a wagon?* But her thoughts turned to other concerns when, a few moments later, they reached the edge of town.

"Well, Lucky, this is Miradero. What do you think?" Jim asked.

She tried to hide her disappointment. Surely there was more to see? She looked to the left, then to the right, but there appeared to be only one main street. "Is this the whole town?"

"Yup," John said. "The whole shebang."

"It won't be like this forever. In a few days we're going to start dynamiting land to lay new railroad track, and before you know it, this will be a bustling city, every bit as good as the one we just left. It will no longer be the end of the line," Jim explained.

But for now it is the end of the line, Lucky thought. She managed a smile so her dad wouldn't sense her frustration. But she wondered: In a place this small, would there be any kids her age?

Jim reached back and patted her hand. "Lucky, keep an open mind. You'll have fun here. I promise." Lucky nodded. Then she gave the town a long look, as if writing a letter to Emma in her mind.

A wide dirt road ran the length of Miradero, which was just two city blocks. Buildings lined both sides of the road. The architecture was a hodgepodge of design, from Spanish stucco, to Western facades, to traditional brick. It was so quiet compared to the city. There were no crowds, no street noise. Only a handful of people walked between the stores. The closest store had a display of cowboy hats in the window. Lucky wondered if Cora would ever trade her pheasant-feathered hat for a cowboy hat. That thought made her giggle.

"Here's the office," John announced, pulling the horses to a stop. Just as Lucky scrambled out of the wagon, a familiar whinnying sound caught her attention. She spun around. The stallion was here, in Miradero! The two men she'd seen earlier were pulling him up the street, their ropes still around his neck. His eyes darted furiously as he fought, kicking and bucking, trying to break free. "Dad, that's him! That's the horse!"

At the sound of her voice, the stallion turned and looked at her, his dark gaze once again meeting hers. For a brief moment, the stallion fell silent. *Does he remember me?* Lucky wondered. Then he turned away and gave another loud whinny. Were those ropes too tight? Was he scared? Lucky felt helpless. "Dad, you said they wouldn't hurt him!"

"They aren't," Jim assured her. "He's just not used to being handled. He'll settle down in a few days."

The men struggled as they guided the stallion farther down the road. His hooves kicked up dirt as he bucked. "He's wild, that's for sure!" one of the men hollered.

"Whoa! Whoa!" shouted the other man as he narrowly avoided being kicked. Then they moved behind a building, disappearing from view. Lucky wanted to run after them. Her legs wanted to sprint around the corner so she could see what was going on.

"Don't even think about it," Cora said as she stepped in front of Lucky. "We just got here and I won't have you taking off already." Lucky frowned. Could Cora actually read her mind? "Besides, that should be a good lesson to you. You see how wild that horse is? That's why I always tell you they are not safe." Then, with a wag of her finger, she said, "You wait *right here.*"

As Jim and Cora stepped into the office of JP & Sons, Lucky stood, staring at the spot where the stallion had kicked up clods of dirt. Her heart ached for him. An hour ago he'd been running free, and now he was here in this strange little town, tied up like a prisoner. He probably felt as out of place as she did.

Lucky was about to follow her dad into the office when a voice said, "Careful or you'll end up smelling like a stable." A girl walked up to Lucky. She pointed at the ground. Lucky had almost stepped in a pile of horse manure.

"Yuck," Lucky said, stepping away. "Thanks for the warning."

The girl smiled at her. The first thing Lucky noticed was the girl's cool blue eyes, so bright in contrast to her dark-red hair. Lucky was immediately relieved to have met another girl, especially one who seemed nice and was about the same age. Cora would very much approve of this girl's clothing. Her button-up blouse had no stains, nor did her gold-buttoned vest. Even her shoes were smudge free, which had to be difficult to maintain with the dusty conditions. "You're Fortuna Prescott, aren't you?" the girl asked.

"Yeah, how did you know?"

"My dad got a telegraph. It said you and your dad were coming out here to live. I hear your dad *owns* the railroad."

"Well, he doesn't exactly *own* it. My grandfather is the one who—"

"I'm Maricela," the girl interrupted. "My father's the mayor." She pointed to a large building looming at the end of the street, decorated with Greek columns and a bell tower. "That's town hall, where *my* dad works. He's in charge of everything." She was clearly bragging, and suddenly Lucky felt as if she were six years old, standing in the schoolyard doing the whole "my dad's better than your dad" thing. Maricela folded her hands behind her back. "So, Fortuna—"

"You can call me Lucky."

"Lucky?" She paused for a moment. "That's an *interesting* name. Don't you like Fortuna?"

"Sure I like it. It's Spanish for 'good fortune.' But my parents started using the nickname Lucky, and it stuck." Maricela narrowed her eyes. Lucky immediately regretted sharing such personal information. She barely knew this girl.

Maricela reached up and adjusted the white silk ribbon that held her long hair away from her face. "Well, *Lucky*, I'm really happy that you're here. Finally, there's someone worth being friends with. You wouldn't believe the kind of kids I've had to put up with in this town." Her smiled faded and her upper lip rose in a sneer. "The worst."

As if on cue, two girls rode their horses down the

street. The first girl had long black hair, pulled back into a single braid. The other girl had blond hair cut in a short bob. Each wore riding pants and a plain shirt. They seemed to be in a hurry and didn't notice Lucky. "Come on," the first girl said. "We've got only a few hours to ride before I gotta do chores."

"Who are they?" Lucky asked.

"Pru Granger and Abigail Stone." Maricela rolled her eyes. "Those two are *not* my friends. All they care about is riding horses. Seriously, that's *all* they do." Then she got that pinched look again, as if she'd eaten a bug. "You don't ride, do you?"

"No," Lucky said. "I'm … I'm not allowed to. My aunt says it's *not appropriate behavior for a young lady of society.*" She mimicked her aunt's stern voice, hoping to get a laugh out of Maricela, because it was silly, really. But Maricela didn't laugh.

"Of course you don't ride." She flipped her hair behind her shoulder. "And why would you? It's stupid. It's beneath people like us. Seriously, I'm so glad to finally have someone who's my equal."

What was that supposed to mean? Was she kidding? Or was she Cora's dream come true?

Suddenly, Lucky got the urge to get as far away from this girl as possible. She'd go see what her dad was doing.

Better yet, Cora was emerging from the office. Surely, Lucky needed to check in with her. "I'd better get—"

"It's official," Maricela said with a delighted clap of her hands. "You are my new best friend. See you at school tomorrow!" With a quick turn on her heel, Maricela marched away, her head held high, her blue skirt swishing.

"What a charming girl," Cora said as she approached.

"Don't you mean what a *snooty* girl?"

"Snooty?" Cora said as she opened her parasol. "Clearly she is a girl of good breeding and education. Look how she's dressed. It gives me hope that this place isn't completely uncivilized."

Jim stuck his head out the office door. "Cora, Lucky, I'm going to stay here for a bit. Looks like we'll need to start dynamiting right away, so there are some details to work out. John will drive you to our new house, and I'll meet you there later."

"Ma'am?" John held out a hand to help Cora into the wagon. He offered to help Lucky, but she'd already climbed onto the front bench. "So, you ready to see your new house?" he asked her.

"Yes!" Lucky said with true enthusiasm. She hoped it would be much nicer than her "new best friend."

14

Cora held tightly to the side of the wagon as the office employee, Mr. John Mercer, drove her and Lucky—and their numerous trunks—to their new home. *This is not a permanent home*, Cora reminded herself. *Just a temporary situation until the railroad is finished.* She would repeat those sentences over and over in her head during the next few days as a way to calm herself when things got tough. *Temporary. Not permanent.*

"Schoolhouse is that way," Mr. Mercer said, pointing down the road. "School starts at eight o'clock. Don't be late or Miss Flores will make you clean the chalkboard." Cora nodded approvingly. Maintaining discipline was important.

The horses took a left at the town hall, then turned again and slowed as they made their way up a hill. Cora's eyelids felt heavy. It had been impossible to sleep on that train. And to make matters worse, her stomach was still unsettled. She just wanted to sit for a moment on something that *wasn't* moving. And this heat was too much. Once she had privacy, she'd take off her boots and stockings and cool off.

"Mr. Mercer, must you hit every rut in the road?" she complained.

"My apologies," Mr. Mercer said kindly. "But please call me John."

"Indeed I won't," Cora told him. How could he suggest such a thing? They barely knew each other. "I will call you Mr. Mercer and you will call me Miss Prescott." She considered educating him on the proper use of titles in various social settings, but that's when a house came into view. Both Cora and Lucky gasped with surprise.

"Wow, is that our house?" Lucky asked as she jumped to her feet.

"Sure is," Mr. Mercer replied.

"Sit down; it's not safe to stand in a moving vehicle," Cora told her. But Lucky had already scrambled out of the wagon and was running toward the house.

It wasn't a stately manor like their home in the city, nor was it a sprawling estate like their house upstate in the country, but charm abounded. It stood three stories high and was painted a cheerful yellow. Two turrets on either side gave it a slightly royal air, like something from a fairy tale. A covered porch, which would thankfully provide plenty of shade, ran along the front. The entire house was accented with white decorative trim in a variety of patterns and shapes. As usual, James Prescott Sr. had spared no expense, wanting to be comfortable no matter where he traveled. A greenbelt of trees peeked out from behind the house, separating it from a craggy outcropping of rocks. Cora realized that the benefit of building the house up here was that it provided a sweeping view of the town. "This will do," she said. It was, in her opinion, the prettiest house in town.

Cora and Lucky carried their smaller trunks to the front porch while Mr. Mercer carried the rest. Once the trunks were all piled on the porch, he told Cora and Lucky that he needed to get back to the office right away. There were boxes of dynamite that had to be counted and then delivered to the work site.

"Thank you, Mr. Mercer," Cora said with a brisk nod.

With a tip of his hat, he rode away, leaving Cora and Lucky to inspect their new residence.

Cora closed her parasol, tucked it under her arm, and took a long breath. "Shall we go inside?" Lucky nodded eagerly. "Oh dear, we don't have a key," Cora realized.

"Maybe we don't need one," Lucky said, reaching out and grabbing the knob. Sure enough, the door swung open. Cora frowned. After seeing all those posters about train robbers and bank robbers, she thought a locked door would be a wise precaution. She made a mental note to discuss security with Jim. But before she could stop Lucky from rushing toward the house, a loud crash sounded. Cora gasped. Her worst nightmare had come true. One of the hooligans was inside!

Cora pulled Lucky away from the door, then drew her parasol like a sword. "Hello?" she called. "We are the Prescotts and this is our home. Whoever you are, you must leave immediately, or I shall summon the authorities!"

Her demand was met with silence.

"Aunt Cora, maybe—"

"*Shhh.*" Cora placed a finger to her lip. They stood, waiting, Cora's parasol poised to strike if need be. Who was in there? Was it more than one robber? Perhaps it would be more efficient to hurry back into town and locate the sheriff, but indignation filled Cora's veins. How dare someone enter her home! It was rude, plain and simple, and she wasn't going to stand for it.

Cora leaned forward, trying to see past the door, which was only halfway open. The front room was filled with crates, each labeled *DELIVER TO THE PRESCOTT HOME, MIRADERO*. Furniture her father had sent years ago, still unpacked because no one had yet lived here. "Hello?" she called again. "Is anyone here?"

Her question was met with a scurrying sound,

like something scratching against the floor. Both she and Lucky shrieked as a small face appeared. Low to the ground and rather round, it waddled toward them. "Heavens," Cora said as she and Lucky backed away from its path. "What on earth is that?" It stopped in the doorway, then looked up at them with its tiny, dark eyes. Its fur was gray and covered with odd spikes.

"It's a porcupine," Lucky said.

"Whatever is it doing in our house? Oh, I do hope it doesn't have a family. Imagine if there are babies and cousins to contend with. Don't get too close. It might be poisonous."

"I'm pretty sure porcupines aren't poisonous. But they can impale you with their quills if they get scared."

"Is that true?" Cora asked.

"Don't you remember last summer, at Grandpa's estate, when the neighbor's hound got a bunch of quills in his nose?"

Cora shuddered. "No one is getting impaled. Not on my watch!" The fact that an animal could stab them with daggers was possibly the most alarming thing Cora had ever heard. "Go!" she told it, accentuating her order with a foot stomp. Fortunately, the creature didn't appear to be the least bit interested in them. It waddled down the front steps and into the yard.

"Good riddance," Cora said. "Now, we must proceed with caution, in case there are more." Parasol still drawn, she was about to go inside when something else appeared in the doorway. It was much smaller than the first creature, and it had sleek black fur and a white stripe running down its back. This time it was Lucky who grabbed Cora and pulled her along the porch.

"Watch out! That's a skunk!" Lucky warned.

Cora opened her parasol, and she and Lucky darted behind it, in case the critter turned its rump at them and sprayed. But it didn't. It scampered down the stairs and disappeared under a hedge. "I'm guessing they don't like us any more than we like them," Lucky noted.

When would this end? How many more beasts would make an appearance? Cora and Lucky waited. But nothing else emerged. "I think that's it," Lucky said after a full minute.

"I certainly hope so. This is the worst welcoming party I've ever witnessed."

"I wonder how they got in," Lucky said as she and Cora cautiously entered their new house for the first time. The answer greeted them immediately. One of the windows had been left open. Not only had critters invaded, but the wind, too, carrying with it enough dust and dirt to cover everything. While charming on the outside, the house's interior was a disaster. The amount of cleaning and unpacking that needed to be done boggled Cora's mind.

"Oh dear." Cora placed her handkerchief to her mouth. "What is that odor?"

"Porcupine poop?" Lucky guessed.

Cora and Lucky explored the house. The first floor included a kitchen, washroom, parlor, dining room, and living room. While most furniture was still crated, a kitchen table and chairs had been unpacked, as had a tall mirror, which leaned against a wall. Upstairs they found three bedrooms. "Oh, can I have this one?" Lucky pleaded. It was built in one of the turrets, with a lovely windowed reading nook.

"Yes, I think this will suit you," Cora said. "That will offer excellent light for homework."

The beds had been set up with mattresses, but they were bare. "There should be linens in these crates, somewhere," Cora said. At her father's request, she'd been the one to order most of the furniture and accessories, hoping to make his home-away-from-home comfortable and cozy. And she'd known that she would make a visit one day; that's why the linens were of a top thread count. "We'll find them later."

"This looks like an attic," Lucky reported from the

topmost floor. "There's nothing up here but a couple of little mice."

Mice? Cora closed her eyes and pressed a finger to her temple. While she was grateful that the train journey had ended, it appeared that another, more complicated journey had begun. It was going to take a great deal of effort to turn this chaos into order.

"Aunt Cora? Can I go outside and explore?"

Cora opened her eyes. Lucky was shuffling back and forth in the doorway as if someone had set a fire under her shoes. "Now is not the time to investigate the outdoors. We have a mess to contend with. It would appear we do not have a housekeeper." Why hadn't her father supplied them with one? This was terrible planning. "So it's a very good thing that I'm here. Tomorrow, my first item of business will be to place a *help wanted* advertisement in the local paper. In the meantime, we'd better start making this place livable."

If Lucky was disappointed by the mess or the lack of organization, she didn't show it. Rather, she searched until she found a broom and a bucket. Then she ran outside to the well for water. Cora looked at the small *gifts* left behind by the porcupine, then at her clean white blouse. Since she rarely did any sort of manual labor, Cora owned no work clothes. But she owned an apron she wore during needlepoint, so she searched through one of her trunks until she found it. She also found a box of tableware and put two of the crisp cloth napkins to work as rags.

Side by side she and Lucky worked, dusting and sweeping, and by the time she began to scrub the floor, she'd given up on trying to keep her dress clean. They'd finished the kitchen and parlor when someone knocked on the front door. Finally, Jim had arrived, but why was he knocking? Cora clenched her jaw. She was going to give him a piece of her mind for leaving them to do all this work!

"Hello?" a woman's voice called.

Cora scrambled to her feet. Who could it possibly be? It was not proper to pay a visit without making prior arrangements. Cora was not prepared with adequate food or beverage. "Hello?" the voice repeated. "I've come to welcome you."

There was no time for Cora to hide her apron, or toss away the wet rag in her hand, or pick the dust balls out of her hair, because the woman barged in.

"Hello. I'm Mrs. Gutierrez, the mayor's wife." She held out a platter of cookies. "These are for you. Welcome to Miradero."

Cora took the platter. "Thank you. I'm Miss Cora Prescott and this is Lucky Prescott."

"Hello." Lucky grabbed a cookie before Cora could stop her. She shoved it into her mouth as if she hadn't eaten in days, though Cora knew this simply wasn't true. Why was her niece always so hungry? "Yum. Did you make these?"

Mrs. Gutierrez snorted. "I don't bake. My housekeeper made them."

"You have a housekeeper?" Cora asked with relief. This was excellent news. "I need to employ one, right away. As soon as possible. Today, perhaps. Is yours available?"

Mrs. Gutierrez looked around. "Yes, you do need help. You poor thing." She patted Cora's arm. "I hate to be the one to break the bad news, but it took us months to find our housekeeper."

"Months?" Cora asked. "Why did it take so long?"

"We placed an advertisement, but then we had to wait and wait and wait. You see, there aren't a lot of people looking to move to a small town like this, and when you find one, well, the train comes out here only twice a month." A train whistle blew out in the distance. "There it goes, heading out. Now you're stuck." She took one of the cookies and delicately nibbled around the edge.

Cora's heart skipped a beat. *Stuck?* Yes, she was

stuck. And it was her own fault. She'd invited herself. She didn't belong in a place like this. How would the Ladies' Social Betterment Society survive without her guidance? What had she done?

But then Cora looked at her niece and her panic subsided. She'd done what she had to do. Lucky needed her, and nothing was more important. The Ladies' Social Betterment Society would have to make do without Cora Prescott for a while.

"If you want to keep up on social news, you have to wait for the big-city newspapers, which are weeks old by the time we get them. And if you want to special-order anything, it can take ages before it finally arrives." Mrs. Gutierrez set the half-nibbled cookie back on the platter. "We get lots of snow in the winter, so you'll need someone to shovel. Do you know how to can tomatoes or make jam? I don't do any of those things, but my housekeeper does. I would be lost without her." An awkward silence followed, during which Cora pondered the reality of her situation. She'd never canned anything in her life.

Mrs. Gutierrez turned her attention to Lucky. "I'm so glad you're here. My daughter tells me you are her new best friend. She doesn't like the other girls in town, and who can blame her? They are cut from ordinary cloth, if you know what I mean."

Lucky gave Mrs. Gutierrez a strange look. "Um, not really," she said with a shrug. Then she held up the linen napkin she'd been using as a rag. "Seems to me a fancy cloth picks up dirt just as good as an *ordinary* cloth." Cora narrowed her eyes at Lucky, warning her to not be rude.

But Mrs. Gutierrez didn't seem to understand Lucky's comment. "My Maricela is special. She's very smart, at the top of the class. She excels in spelling, geometry, and diction."

"Diction is most important," Cora said. "I always tell Lucky, when you speak, do so clearly and with confidence."

"That is good motherly advice," Mrs. Gutierrez said.

"Oh, she's not my mother," Lucky told her, carefully wiping cookie crumbs from the corner of her mouth. "She's my aunt."

"I see." Mrs. Gutierrez looked around. "And where is your mother?"

"She...she died," Lucky said. "When I was two." Cora had heard Lucky answer that question many times before, but the unfair reality still stung. And the realization that ten years had already passed shocked her.

"I see," Mrs. Gutierrez said in a matter-of-fact way. "Well, these things happen, don't they?" Her expression was blank. She'd shown more emotion when mentioning tomato canning.

Cora didn't want Lucky to be made uncomfortable by Mrs. Gutierrez's uncaring reaction, so she decided to change the subject. "Tell me, Mrs. Gutierrez, what sort of clubs do you have? I was the treasurer for the Ladies' Social Betterment Society back home, and I served on the Art Selection Committee for the museum."

"We have nothing like that here," she replied with a sigh. "Well, good day." And just as quickly as she had barged in, she retreated, her skirt sashaying as she made her way down the driveway.

No social betterment clubs? Cora turned and caught her reflection in the mirror. "Oh my word!" she exclaimed. Her hair was a tangled mess, her face was streaked with dirt—what had the mayor's wife thought?

"Uh-oh, Aunt Cora, you're not going to like this!" Lucky called. "Shoo! Shoo!"

"Oh for goodness sake, what is it now?" Cora hurried into the kitchen, where Lucky was trying to pull the parasol out of a goat's mouth.

"I accidentally left the kitchen door open," she explained. "And he wandered in. Hey, stop eating that." With a groan and a tug, Lucky finally pulled the parasol free. But it had been shredded. The goat bleated at them. Lucky shooed it with the broom, then shut the door.

Cora Prescott examined the ruined parasol, then sank onto a chair. "What have I done?" she mumbled, wishing she'd made her escape with that porcupine and skunk. The sound of the train's final good-bye whistle echoing off the mountains made her feel even worse.

15

Night had fallen by the time Jim joined them at the house. He brought groceries and a big dose of enthusiasm, which both Lucky and Cora needed after hours of cleaning. He showed his sister how to start a fire in the stove and how to use the griddle, a skill he'd learned in his bachelor days on the ranch. They fried eggs and ate tortillas, Lucky's new favorite food. For dessert there were dried plums and the rest of the cookies.

Lucky couldn't stop thinking about tomorrow. Her first day of school. What if Maricela was right? What if the other girls were...*the worst*?

Jim talked between bites—and during bites, which would normally drive Cora mad, but she seemed too tired to notice. It had been a long afternoon. Lucky hadn't minded the hard work; it had been a welcome distraction. And she'd been surprised by Cora's willingness to get down on the floor and scrub. And scoop critter poop. Who would have thought?

"Jim!" Cora finally blurted, bringing his long monologue to an end. "I'm glad things went well at the office. However, there are important matters to tend to. This house is a mess."

He set his fork aside. "Looks pretty good to me."

"Dad, that's only because Aunt Cora and I cleaned. You should have seen the place."

"There were wild animals in here, Jim!" Cora's exhaustion began leaking out the corners of her eyes in the form of tears.

"There, there," Jim said. He leaned across the table and kissed his sister's cheek. "I'm sorry. I will help you as much as I can. I'll start unpacking the furniture."

Jim first focused on Cora's room so she could call it a day and get some sleep. Then he carried a dresser into Lucky's room, along with a bedside table and lamp.

"Settling in okay?" he asked.

Lucky was sitting on the floor, riffling through one of her trunks. "It's weird," she said, pulling out her old stuffed bear. "Even though my things are the same, it still doesn't feel like home."

"You know, the West is your home—your first home, since it's where I met your mom and where you were born." He reached into the trunk and pulled out the framed circus flyer. He hung it next to her bed. "You loved it back then."

"I was two. I don't remember that."

"Well, you'll just have to take my word for it." He nudged her, trying to get a smile, but Lucky felt so unsure about everything. "What's the matter? Are you worried about school?"

"I've never been the new girl before. What if…what if no one likes me?"

"That's impossible! How could anyone not like you?"

"Dad," she grumbled. His giant grin wasn't making her feel better. "You're not taking this seriously." Didn't he know that there were countless things that could go wrong? What if no one wanted to sit with her at lunch? What if she couldn't stop fidgeting, and she got in trouble on the first day? What if that snobby Maricela was the nicest person in town?

Jim gazed at the poster. "You know, your mom had lots of friends in the village where she grew up, but even though she loved them, she wasn't happy."

"Why not?"

"She wanted her life to be bigger. So she left behind everything and everyone she knew and came out West, all by herself. And you know what? It was the best thing that ever happened to her…or to me. Or to you!" He sat on the edge of the bed. Lucky sat next to him. "Your mother was alone when she came West, but you're not. You have me and you have your aunt."

Lucky nodded. But she still couldn't manage a smile. It had been easier to look happy back in the city, before they'd actually left, because Miradero had felt unreal. Like a story. But now it was real. This house. This town. The new school.

"I don't think I'm as brave as Mom was." Lucky hung her head.

"Of course you are," Jim said. "You know how you're always asking me what you and your mom have in common?" Lucky looked up and nodded. "And how I always say that you look just like her?" She nodded again. "Well, I think you are brave, too. You wanted to come out here, remember? That's very brave. So now all you need to do is to give Miradero a shot. Deal?" He held out his pinkie.

There were a few things in this world that Lucky could not abide. Bullying. The mistreatment of animals. And disappointing her father. "Deal." She wrapped her pinkie around his and they shook. *What are you made of?* Madame Barrow had asked. Lucky wanted the answer to be "bravery." *I am brave. Brave like my mother.*

The moment was long and peaceful, interrupted only by a strange sound coming from the next room. "What was that?"

"That, sweet pea, is your Aunt Cora. Apparently, she

snores." He chuckled. "But we won't tell her. She'd be mortified."

After a kiss good night, Jim left Lucky alone in her room, the door slightly ajar. Even though it had been an incredibly long day, and even though her body was weary, she couldn't yet quiet her mind. School days were always the same back home. She'd get up, put on her uniform, and go downstairs for breakfast with Mr. and Mrs. MacFinn and her dad. Then Mrs. MacFinn would escort her to school. She'd have recitations, then tea, then library, followed by math and lunch, then history. Scheduled. Predictable. But what would it be like here?

Lucky walked over to the reading nook and opened the window. She'd never seen so many stars. She leaned on the sill to get a better view. The town lay in stillness, no signs of people or wagons moving about. An owl hooted from a nearby tree. A campfire sparkled in the distance. And surrounding it all, those tabletop mountains, dark silhouettes beneath the bright, starry sky. One last thought crossed her mind before a yawn led her to bed.

Was the stallion missing his old home as much as she was missing hers?

16

Down the hill from the yellow house, beyond Lucky's view, the stallion stood, his eyes gazing at the night sky. He'd fought hard, but the men and their ropes had overpowered him, and now he was to spend the night surrounded by a fence. He'd tried to jump, but the space was too small to build up speed. Fortunately, the rest of his herd had run far away and were safe. The stallion's legs ached. His shoulders felt weary. He wanted to lie down and rest, but he wouldn't let them see his exhaustion. He would never bend to their will. He stood tall, head held high.

Nothing had been able to hold him. Not the river, when he'd fallen in as a foal. It had tried to sweep him away, but he'd battled against the current, swimming until he'd reached safety.

Not the ice, when he'd stepped onto that pond last winter, believing the ground was solid, only to have it crack under his hooves. Despite the freezing temperatures, he'd fought until he was free.

And not the wind, which had blown sand across the prairie last summer, making it impossible for the stallion to see his way home. But he'd waited for the storm to pass, and then he'd found his way.

And now it would be men who'd learn the truth. Try as they might, they'd lose this battle. The stallion would find his way out.

A soft whinny drew his attention. His sister stood on the other side of the fence, her eyes filled with worry and fear. He pushed against the fence, showing her that he was captive. She paced back and forth, assessing the situation. She chewed on the gate, trying to loosen the latch with her teeth. It was no use.

"I'll be right back. Gonna check on the stallion," a man said in the distance.

The stallion's ears flicked. His sister's eyes widened. She pulled her head from the fence and turned in the direction of the man's voice. Footsteps sounded, moving closer. Someone was coming. The stallion turned to his sister. He stomped his hoof. *Go!* But she looked at him, pleadingly, so desperately wanting to help. The footsteps were drawing nearer. Any moment now, a man would appear—a man with ropes. The stallion let loose a high-pitched neigh. *GO!*

With one last look, a look that said *I love you* and *Good-bye* at the same time, the filly made her escape, her hooves pounding until they faded into the dark night.

For the stallion, this was not good-bye. For he was determined to be free.

Part Three

17

Lucky sat in her grandfather's private box,
perched high above the opera house stage. Though
the hall's lights had been dimmed, it was easy to see
fellow audience members, thanks to a ring of fire that
burned smack-dab in the center of the stage. As Lucky
squeezed the armrests of her chair, she almost forgot to
breathe. The show was about to begin.

The audience hushed as Cowgirl Betty, sitting atop
her black stallion, Shadow, made her entrance. Just as
before, Shadow wore feathers in his mane and a beautiful
red blanket on his back. Betty wore her cowgirl hat, her
red bandana, and fringed pants. With a swing of her leg,
she slid out of the saddle, then waved her hat at the
audience. Everyone cheered. Lucky tightened her grip on
the armrests, her jaw clenching with anticipation. Were
they going to do it? Were Betty and Shadow actually
going to jump through that ring of fire?

But rather than getting back onto her horse, Betty
did something strange. She reached out her hand, and
suddenly Lucky found herself standing on the stage.
Confused, she spun around. The ring was directly
behind her, its flames licking the air. She spun back

around. Hundreds of upturned faces, cast in flickering orange light, stared at her from the seats.

"What am I doing here?" Lucky asked.

Betty smiled at her. "You're gonna show everyone what you're made of." She plopped her hat onto Lucky's head and in an instant, Lucky was sitting in the saddle. Cowgirl Betty led Shadow to a position at the edge of the stage, then turned him to face the fire. She handed the reins to Lucky and stepped away. Lucky's entire body tensed. Wait, was Shadow going to jump with her on his back? But Lucky had no training. This was impossible!

Or was it?

Show them what you're made of.

With a tight grip on the reins, she opened her mouth to give the command, but all that came out was, "Lucky!" Up in the private box seat, Aunt Cora wagged a finger. "You get down here this instant or you'll be late for school!"

School? Lucky's eyes flew open.

As if a twister had suddenly touched down in Lucky's bedroom, the covers flew off the bed, a bathrobe was yanked from its hook, and a blur of color dashed down the stairs. "What time is it?" Lucky asked as she pushed her tangled hair from her eyes. "Am I late?"

"Hey, take a breath, sweet pea. You're not late. You've

got plenty of time to eat breakfast." Jim was already dressed and seated at the kitchen table, a cup of coffee in hand. "Your aunt has been working hard this morning. She's made our first official breakfast in our new home."

The kitchen looked as if the twister had touched there, too. Eggshells, flour, and sugar were strewn across the counter. Every bowl and spoon that had been unpacked the night before was now dirty. And Cora stood in the middle of the chaos, with dollops of batter clinging to her hair and apron. "You can't go to school without a nutritious meal," she said. Then she set a platter of pancakes in the middle of the table. Lucky was surprised that the cakes looked so perfect.

But what would they taste like? She gave her dad a long *You go first* look.

While Lucky and Cora watched, Jim selected a pancake, set it on his plate, and politely took a bite. He chewed very slowly, then swallowed. "Yum," he said with surprise. "Delicious."

Cora narrowed her eyes at him. "Jim Prescott, are you humoring me? Cooking on a wood-burning stove is very difficult."

"No, not at all. They're great."

Lucky sat, grabbed a plate and napkin, then ate a whole pancake. "Thanks, Aunt Cora," she said. Cora smiled proudly. Lucky poured herself a glass of cider, her legs swinging as she drank. "Someone's in a good mood," Jim said.

"Yep. I've decided to keep a positive outlook. I'm really excited about starting school and making some new friends."

"That's my girl." Jim took another sip of coffee, then got up and grabbed his coat. "I've got to head out. We've a ton of work to do today." He kissed Cora on the cheek. "Thanks for breakfast." Then he kissed Lucky on the top of her head. "Good luck. Can't wait to hear all about your first day."

"Can't wait to hear about *your* first day," Lucky told him. With that, Jim hurried out the door and down the long driveway to town.

Lucky set her plate in the sink, then took the stairs two at a time. She searched through her wardrobe. Did they have uniforms at this school? If not, what did the kids wear? Maricela had been in a nice dress with a hair ribbon, but those other two girls had been wearing riding pants and shirts. Lucky didn't own any pants. She riffled through one of her trunks, tossing clothes here and there. John Mercer had said that formal clothes weren't needed, that it was casual dress hereabouts. Lucky sighed. Why were all her clothes so fancy?

"You have only one chance to make a good first impression," Cora said as she picked a dress off the floor. "You're going to wear this."

The dress she'd selected just happened to be the frilliest, flounciest dress Lucky owned—light-pink, with a pattern of dark-pink flowers, and layer upon layer of ruffles cascading from the waist to the hem.

"No way. I'm not wearing that."

The Prescott tendency toward stubbornness was never more evident than when Lucky and Cora stood, face-to-face, in disagreement with each other. Each face painted with determination, chin out, arms folded, unwavering and unblinking. Lucky knew that she and Cora would both stand there all day just to make a point. But Lucky didn't have all day. School would be starting soon. And she'd promised her dad that she'd be brave.

"Fine," Lucky grumbled, snatching the dress from her aunt's hands. Cora smiled with victorious satisfaction.

About ten minutes later, when Lucky made her way back downstairs, she took one stair at a time so her legs wouldn't get tangled in all the silk layers. Aunt Cora clapped her hands with delight. "You look lovely!" She tied a ribbon around the end of Lucky's braid. Then she handed Lucky a small leather satchel.

"What's this?"

"Well, you're not going to believe it," Cora said. "When I was getting water from the pump, I saw a neighbor across the way, feeding her chickens, so I asked her about the school, and she filled me in. Things are much rougher than we ever imagined. You are expected to bring your own lunch." At Madame Barrow's Finishing School for Young Ladies, lunch was prepared by the cook and served in a dining room on china plates. Cora pointed to the satchel. "It's not a gourmet feast, mind you; I did my best with the groceries your father provided. Let's go."

Cora had cleaned the batter from her hair. She and Lucky began to walk down the driveway toward town. Lucky glanced at the shrubbery. No sign of porcupines or skunks today. The air was already warm, but not hot like yesterday, thanks to a smattering of puffy clouds.

They reached the main road. A boy walked ahead of them, a leather bag flung over his shoulder. Two girls, much younger than Lucky, walked together, baskets swinging from their hands. Lucky realized that none of the other kids were walking with an adult. She stopped, turned to her aunt, and said, "Aunt Cora, I can do the rest on my own."

Cora was about to object, but she surprised Lucky

by nodding. "I'd like to take a bath before I meet people," she said, wiping flecks of flour from her arm. "And change into a nicer dress." She adjusted Lucky's ribbon, then smoothed one of the ruffles. "Okay. Well, I guess this is it. Go on, now." As she stepped back, she wrung her hands. Was Cora as nervous as Lucky? Even though Lucky was still sore about having to wear the ridiculous pink dress, she gave her aunt a quick kiss on the cheek.

"Bye," Lucky said.

Trying not to kick up dirt on the dusty road, Lucky followed the other kids toward the schoolhouse. Never before had she been allowed to walk to school unchaperoned. She took this as a good sign of things to come. But then she looked down at her dress. The ruffles expanded with each step, the layers rising and falling as if she were about to take flight. "Some first impression I'm going to make," she mumbled.

The walk to school wasn't very long. It took Lucky past Town Hall, where a group of men stood on the steps, engaged in a heated discussion about the price of hay. To her right was the mayor's home, with its stately veranda and walkway. A woman in an apron tended to a small flower patch in front of the house. Lucky followed the two young girls as they took a left, passing a sprawling ranch. A sign hung between two fence posts. GRANGER

RAMADA. A flat-front building stood on the right, with the sign BLACKSMITH hanging above its entry. Wagon wheels leaned against the exterior walls, and the front doors were wide open, revealing a fire burning in a stone pit. Sounds of clanking drifted from the shop. Lucky continued walking. The sights were so different from the ones in the city. No newsboys calling out headlines. No customers sitting in sidewalk cafés. The pace was slow. The air so quiet she could hear a squirrel as it chattered at her from a nearby tree. She smiled when she came to a corral.

About a dozen horses stood inside a circular fence. Some were drinking water, others were standing about. A few playfully nudged one another, clearly friends. But one horse stood by himself in a separate, smaller corral, his back turned to the others. He seemed familiar, with his golden tan color, black mane, black tail, and black legs. Lucky's heart skipped a beat. *Could it be?* While the other kids continued to school, Lucky walked around the fence until she could see the horse's face. A white stripe ran down his nose. It was him. The wild mustang. The stallion!

"Hey, fella," she said. He moved away, keeping his back turned. She followed him. "What's the matter, boy? Don't you remember me from the train?"

The stallion lifted his head and glanced at her. He gave a little snort. Did he recognize her? For a moment she was certain he did, but then he turned away again. She stepped onto the fence's lower board, then to the middle board, so he could better see her. "I'm sorry you're all cooped up in here."

His ears flicked in her direction. He *was* listening. How could she keep his attention? Maybe there was something in her lunch. She jumped back onto the ground and opened her satchel. A sandwich, cookie, and apple were nestled inside. "Would this help you feel better?" Forgetting about her fancy dress, she knelt next to the fence and reached her arm between two fence boards, the apple resting in her upturned palm. The stallion gave a quick glance. His nostrils flared. Was he picking up the apple's scent? Surely he'd want to eat it. No horse can resist the juicy sweetness of an apple.

But he turned away. Lucky's shoulders slumped. He didn't trust her. Why should he? The other people had caught him with ropes. How could she prove to him that she wouldn't hurt him? She took a bite of the apple. "*Mmmmm.* It's so good. Are you sure you don't want it?"

His nostrils flared again and he looked at her. Then he took a hesitant step in her direction. She moved her palm up and down. "It's okay, fella, I'm not gonna hurt you. You're all right." He took another cautious step, then another, slowly moving closer. *Maybe he bites*, Lucky warned herself. *Maybe I shouldn't be sticking my hand out like this.* But as she weighed the risk of losing her fingers against the thrill of feeding a wild mustang, the stallion lowered his neck and reached with his teeth. Lucky slowly pulled her hand back, trying to coax him closer. The fruit's scent had clearly entranced him, because his eyes were focused on the shiny red apple. He stepped closer, still trying to get a nibble. When he was close enough, Lucky reached out and gently tapped him on the chin. "Boop," she said with a playful laugh. Startled, the stallion lifted his head. Lucky tossed the apple at him and he caught it in midair. Then he devoured it. "Guess you needed that," she said.

He watched her for a moment. Before she could react, he dipped his head and grabbed her sandwich out of the leather bag.

"Hey," she said with another laugh. Lucky didn't even know what kind of sandwich it was, but he seemed to like it. She couldn't believe he was standing so close to her. This gorgeous creature who'd been running across the prairie was here, in front of her. How she longed to pet him just once.

Bong. Bong.

Both Lucky and the stallion turned toward the sound of a bell ringing.

"Oops, I'd better get to school." Lucky didn't want to leave the stallion, but her new life was about to start. A new day, with new friends. She scrambled to her feet and wiped dirt from her dress. Cora wasn't going to be happy about the stains. "Well, good-bye," she said. She started to leave, then noticed how all the other horses were still hanging out together, far away from the stallion. "Tell you what," she said, climbing back onto the fence. He cocked his head, listening attentively to her every word. "I'm gonna make lots of friends today. And so should you." He snorted and shook his head. "I know, but we're both stuck here. So we might as well make the best of it. I promise to try if you promise to try. Okay?"

He moved closer to her. Did he want her to pet him? Turned out, she'd forgotten about her lunch satchel, which still lay open on the ground. "Hey," she said as he grabbed the cookie. Then he trotted around the corral in triumph. She might have been angry, but all she could do was laugh. He was quite the skilled thief. She jumped off the fence, grabbed her satchel, then waved good-bye.

"Remember our promise!" she called out to him. Then, lifting the hem of her skirt, Lucky ran the rest of the way to school.

18

The stallion watched the girl as she ran away. He neighed at her, wanting her to come back, because her gifts had been delicious. He'd eaten apples many times, but where had she found those other foods? Did they grow nearby? He wanted more.

While his stomach had appreciated the girl's visit, there was another reason he longed for her return. Her voice had soothed him, the way cricket song did, or the soft patter of rain. When the girl spoke, he didn't feel so scared, even though he was captured and imprisoned behind a fence. But, alas, that was where he found himself. No matter how hard he pushed, the gate would not open. He flicked his tail, trying to get rid of an annoying fly. Then he rubbed his flank against a post, working on an itch.

"Pasture time!"

The stallion stopped scratching and tensed. A man opened the gate in the larger corral and began ushering the other horses outside. Was he letting them go? The stallion snorted, expectantly, for surely he would be next. Surely they'd let him return to his herd. The stallion neighed, high and tense, demanding the man's attention.

"Don't worry," the man called to him. "Mr. Granger will be out to deal with you." He patted a few of the horses on the flank. They playfully nudged him as they walked past. He even pressed his face against a white horse's face. "Good girl," he said.

Why did those other horses allow him to touch them? Why did they follow him willingly?

Once the horses had disappeared from view, the man took something from his pocket, drank from it, then leaned against the fence. The stallion hadn't had anything to drink in a while. He'd refused the offers of water and oats from his captors. The girl, however—she'd been different. She hadn't locked him up.

A second man leaned against the fence. Now there were two, staring at the stallion as if they'd never seen a horse before. Frustrated, the stallion was about to turn his back to them when a third man appeared, this one taller and wider than the others.

"You two are new, so I'm gonna explain to you how this works. Listen up."

"Yes, sir, Mr. Granger," they both said.

The taller man opened the gate and stepped into

the small corral. The gate clicked shut behind him. The stallion watched warily. "When you first get yourself a wild horse, you gotta put him in a small, round corral. Why do you think that is?"

The other two men shrugged.

"'Cause there ain't no corners. You see? You don't want the mustang putting his head in the corner, 'cause that means his backside is facing you. And you never want his backside facing you. Mustangs can kick real good." He lifted his shirt and pointed to his belly.

"*Whoo-eee*, that's some scar, Mr. Granger."

"And you want the corral to be small so he can exercise, but he can't build up enough speed to jump out," the tall man said.

"That makes sense."

"Since today's the first day with this stallion, we're gonna take it easy. We gotta build his trust and that takes time." The taller man took a step forward. The stallion tensed again, and took two steps back. A rope hung from the man's hand. "It's okay, boy. I'm not gonna hurt you." He stepped closer. The stallion began to move around the inside edge of the fence. There was nowhere to go. Only around and around. There wasn't enough room to break into a gallop, so he trotted.

The tall man stood in the center of the corral. "You

see what I'm doing?" he asked the other two. "I'll talk to him, real gentle, but I'll let him circle until he gets tired. Tired is good. It'll make him less ornery."

The stallion kept trotting, but there was no place to go. Why was the man standing there, watching him? Why was he smiling?

"If they're young, like this one, they get tired easier," the tall man said.

"He don't look like he's getting tired," the second man said.

The stallion didn't like the way the tall man was looking at him. It was a look of challenge. A look of threat. The stallion headed straight for the tall man. "Whoa!" The man turned tail and ran, flinging himself back over the fence, his hat flying. The stallion reared and neighed, but this time it was the sound of victory.

"You okay, Mr. Granger?" the first man asked, helping the taller man to his feet.

"That mustang's a real wild one. You really think he can be broken?" the second man asked.

The taller man wiped dirt off his palms. "It's just a matter of time," he said, placing his hat back on his head. "Every horse can be broken." His gaze met the stallion's, their eyes equally ablaze with stubbornness and determination. Then the three men walked away.

Even though he was alone in the corral, the stallion reared and bucked. Thirst burned his throat and exhaustion weighed down his muscles, but he reared again. He would not be like those other horses.

He would *never* be broken.

19

For Abigail Stone it was a regular sort of morning.
She rode her horse to school alongside her best friend,
Pru Granger. And because Snips, her six-year-old
brother, loved riding but wasn't ready for a big horse of
his own, she let him climb into the front of her saddle so
he wouldn't have to walk. She even let him take the reins
for a short while. Snips was wiggly, but Abigail's horse
was patient and mostly ignored the kicking.

When they got to school, Abigail and Pru led their
horses, Boomerang and Chica Linda, into the school's
small corral. They removed the saddles and reins and
grabbed their brushes from the saddlebags. Brushing
a horse was hard work, and Abigail's arms were getting
really strong. But there were only a few minutes until
school began, so the brushing was quick. Abigail made
sure the trough was filled with water. Pru got a scoop
of oats to keep the horses happy. After some smooches
and hugs, which the horses loved, they said good-bye.
Then the girls climbed the front steps into the little
schoolhouse. It was a pretty building, painted brick-red
with white trim. They set their lunch baskets on a shelf,
then walked to their seats. The first thing Abigail heard

was Maricela talking. And talking. Which was Maricela's favorite thing to do.

Only on this morning, Maricela actually had something new to say.

"I met her yesterday," Maricela told a few other students who'd gathered around her.

"Who?" Abigail asked.

Maricela smiled proudly, for she loved it when she knew stuff no one else knew. This happened often since her father was the mayor, and he received important news over the telegraph. "I met the new girl," Maricela said. "She's from the city. You should have seen it. They had about twenty trunks. Daddy says her father is a railroad baron, which means she's a cut above. I'm so happy I finally have an equal to socialize with."

Pru looked at Abigail and rolled her eyes. If anyone could get under Pru's skin, it was Maricela. "'Cut above,'" Pru said. "That's insulting."

"Well, it's true," Maricela told her. "Anyway, she's my new best friend."

Bong. Bong. The school bell rang again. Miss Flores, the teacher, emerged from the stairwell that led to the little bell tower. Abigail loved most everything about Miss Flores. She was the kindest teacher, and she always let the girls run outside to check on their horses. Her hair was a mix of blond and red. Abigail's mother called it 'strawberry blond.'

As Miss Flores shuffled through some papers on her desk, the students began to take their seats. There were four rows of desks in the Miradero schoolhouse. Abigail and Pru always sat next to each other, except for the days when Miss Flores had to separate them because they were giggling too much. Pru had been Abigail's best friend her whole life. They'd celebrated birthdays together. They'd had sleepovers together. They'd even learned how to ride horses together. It never bothered Abigail that Pru was a much better rider. Abigail just loved being outside on her horse. But those difficult trails, the ones Pru preferred, were not her favorites.

"I hope the new girl isn't as stuck-up as Maricela," Pru whispered to Abigail.

Abigail hoped the same thing. There were very few kids her age in Miradero, and having a new girl would be so much fun. But the way Maricela was talking, it sounded as if this girl wouldn't want to hang out with Abigail and Pru. There was always a chance Maricela was wrong. "You know how Maricela likes to brag," Abigail whispered back. "Maybe the girl is nice."

"Everyone, take your seats," Miss Flores said.

"Snips," Abigail called. She motioned to her brother

to stop rolling his marble on the floor and to take his seat. This was his first year at school, and she'd promised their mother that she'd keep an eye on him since he tended to wander off. And break things.

"Aw, can't I just—"

"Snips," she urged again. With a pout, he stuck the marble in his pocket. But instead of getting into his chair, he stared at the doorway. The room fell into silence as everyone turned in that direction.

A girl stood there. She didn't move. She didn't say anything. She seemed unsure of what to do next. "What is she wearing?" Pru whispered.

Abigail had been wondering the same thing. The girl's pink dress filled the entire doorway. Abigail had never seen so many ruffles. It was like something she'd only read about, like what Cinderella might wear to the ball. "It's the most beautiful dress in the world," she said.

Miss Flores stepped out from behind her desk to greet the girl. "Hello. I'm Miss Flores, your teacher. You must be Fortuna Prescott."

Fortuna, what a pretty name, Abigail thought.

"Actually, she prefers to be called Lucky. All her *real* friends call her Lucky." Maricela smiled smugly. Abigail thought that Lucky was an even prettier name than Fortuna. "I know all about her name because—"

"Yeah, we get it, Maricela," Pru said with a groan. "You know *everything*."

Because Lucky looked frozen in place, Miss Flores gently placed her hand on Lucky's back and guided her toward the front of the room. "Please come in. Why don't you tell us a little about yourself?"

Lucky's cheeks went red. She looked around. Everyone was seated, including Snips, so all eyes were staring at her. She swallowed hard, then began. "Well, um, I'm twelve."

"Oh, that's the same age as me and Pru," Abigail said happily.

"And me," Maricela added.

Lucky continued. "My dad, my aunt, and I arrived yesterday. On the train."

"Her dad *owns* the railroad," Maricela interrupted.

"Why don't you let her talk?" Pru snapped.

"Yes, Maricela, we know that you're excited to welcome our new student, but let's give Lucky a chance to talk." Miss Flores often encouraged Maricela to *be quiet*.

Maricela folded her arms and made her signature *hmmphf* sound.

"My dad doesn't *own* the railroad," Lucky explained. "My grandfather does. My dad works for him. He's going to help build the line from Miradero to the ocean."

"How come you're dressed like a princess?" Snips asked.

Lucky's cheeks turned even redder. "I…I…" She looked down at her feet. "I wasn't sure what to wear. We wore uniforms at my old school. Madame Barrow's Finishing School for Young Ladies." Someone snickered.

"What are they finishing?" a boy asked.

"Um…" Lucky hesitated. "Madame Barrow always says that she's trying to turn us into works of art." More snickering.

Abigail didn't like it that people were laughing at the new girl. "It's a pretty dress," she said.

Pru raised her hand. "Can I ask a question?"

"*May* you ask a question," Miss Flores corrected. "And yes, you may."

"How did you ride to school in a dress like that?"

"Ride to school? You mean, on a horse?" Pru nodded. Lucky shuffled in place. "I didn't ride here, I walked, just like back home. Mrs. MacFinn and I always walked together, even in the rain."

"Who's Mrs. MacFinn?" Abigail asked.

"She's our…" Lucky looked around and gulped again. "Housekeeper."

"Housekeeper? Yup, total snob," Pru whispered to Abigail.

Abigail sighed. Uniforms, housekeeper, a school for young ladies. It did seem as if Lucky was very different from them. Maybe Maricela was right.

"Well, Lucky, we are very happy to have you here with us. Why don't you take that empty desk?" Miss Flores said. The desk just happened to be on the end of the row, right next to Pru.

"Can't she sit next to me?" Maricela asked. "We have so much in common."

"I'm sure Lucky will be fine next to Pru. Okay, everyone, open your math books." Miss Flores handed Lucky a brand-new book.

"Thank you," Lucky said. It was a bit of a struggle for her to fit behind her desk, what with all those layers of fabric, but she managed. Abigail wondered if she could borrow that dress one day. But then she remembered the "cut above" comment and frowned. With a disappointed sigh, she opened her book.

The morning moved along at a snail's pace, with Abigail sneaking glances at the new girl now and then. Lucky wore her brown hair in a long braid, just like Pru. And she seemed quick at her work, solving math equations faster than anyone else. At every opportunity, Maricela sauntered over to Lucky, whispering things in her ear. They certainly seemed like best friends.

"Lunchtime," Miss Flores announced. "Be back in twenty minutes."

"Finally," Pru said. "My stomach's growling like a cornered badger." She pushed back her chair and hurried into the mudroom. Abigail followed. With lunch sacks in hand, they ran down the stairs, straight to their horses. Boomerang and Chica Linda were waiting expectantly. Abigail loved Boomerang with all her heart. He was the nicest horse she'd ever met, and the goofiest, too. He was brown with large white patches, and no matter how often she tried to tame his forelock, it always seemed to hang in his face. While Boomerang was handsome in a sweet way, Chica Linda was beautiful. Golden in color, with a white mane and white tail, she had the longest eyelashes of any horse Abigail had ever seen. And just like Abigail and Pru, these two horses were the best of friends.

After the girls checked to make sure there was enough water in the trough, it was time to eat lunch. The girls claimed their favorite spot under the oak tree. Abigail opened her lunch sack. It was her job to make lunch for Snip and herself, so she'd made their favorite— blueberry jam sandwiches, carrot sticks, and apple wedges. Pru had a hearty chicken salad sandwich and enough oatmeal cookies to share.

"I heard one of Dad's ranch hands talking about some

arrowheads he found," Pru said. "I'm gonna find out where he got them and maybe we can go."

"That would be fun," Abigail said. Pru always had great ideas for adventures. As Abigail munched on a carrot stick, she noticed that Lucky was sitting on a bench with Maricela on the other side of the schoolyard. Maricela was talking a mile a minute. Lucky was listening, but she wasn't laughing or smiling. How come she wasn't eating? Didn't she have food? Abigail thought about offering her some apple wedges, but then Lucky got up and wandered over to the fence. Chica Linda eagerly presented her neck for a good rub. Then Boomerang jealously pushed Chica Linda aside, trying to get all the attention.

"Don't worry," Lucky said with a laugh. "I've got two hands." She pet both horses. This surprised Abigail. While Boomerang loved everyone, Chica Linda was picky and could take a while to warm up to a stranger. But there she was, letting this new girl stroke her neck.

Abigail nudged Pru with her elbow. "Look at what she's doing. Maybe she's not so bad after all. Let's go talk to her."

Pru didn't look super pleased with the idea, but she willingly followed Abigail over to the fence. "Hi, I'm Pru and this here's Abigail."

"I like your hair ribbon," Abigail said.

"Thanks. These are nice horses," Lucky told them.

"That's Chica Linda; she's mine," Pru said. At the sound of her name, Chica Linda stomped her front hoof and proudly shook her mane.

"And that's Boomerang; he belongs to me. He's a goofball, but I love him." At the sound of his name, Boomerang nickered.

"What kind of horses are these?" Lucky asked.

Abigail gave Boomerang a gentle push because he'd started chewing on Lucky's braid. "He's a pinto. Pru's horse is a palomino. She's won a dozen blue ribbons already."

"So, do you have a horse?" Pru asked.

"No, I don't ride."

"You mean you don't ride to school, like you told us," Abigail said.

Lucky frowned at her feet. "I mean, I don't ride at all. I never have."

"Of course she doesn't ride. She wouldn't be caught dead on a horse." Maricela was interrupting, as usual. She squeezed in next to Lucky. "Horses aren't for people like us. *Society* people."

Pru snorted. "Yeah? We'll you're wrong about that, Maricela. *Society people*, as you put it, have always loved horses. How do you think kings and queens traveled? And haven't you ever heard of polo? Who do you think plays that, peasants?"

Maricela ignored her. "The only reason Lucky was petting your horses is that she was being polite."

Pru frowned at Lucky. "Sorry you feel that way. Come on, Abigail."

Lucky stammered. "Wait, I...I..."

They didn't hang around to hear what Lucky had to say. Abigail had to scurry to keep up with Pru's angry pace. *How disappointing*, Abigail thought. How fun it would have been to add a new friend to their mix, but apparently it wasn't meant to be.

20

"Why would you say that to them?" Lucky asked Maricela as Abigail and Pru hurried away. "Now they think I'm some stuck-up snob who hates horses."

"Who cares? They're dirty, smelly animals." Maricela snickered. "And their horses aren't much better."

For a moment, Lucky felt completely baffled. She couldn't believe what she'd just heard. Dirty and smelly? She waited for the mayor's daughter to say she was just teasing, the way people do when they've made a really bad joke. But Maricela stood there, beaming with pride, as if she thought herself clever with her insulting turn of phrase. Was she waiting for Lucky to agree?

Things had been going so well. The horses had seemed to like her. She, Abigail, and Pru had been chatting like friends. But then Maricela had barged into the conversation and ruined everything.

Maricela was horrid.

Lucky stared at her, unsure what to do next. Making an enemy on the first day of school certainly wasn't what she'd hoped for when she'd left the house that morning. But being part of a mean-girl duo wasn't what she'd wanted, either. "Maricela, I don't think it's nice to call *anyone* dirty and smelly."

Because they were no longer getting attention, Boomerang and Chica Linda trotted over to their water trough, but as they did, a fleck of dirt flew into the air and landed right on Maricela's dress. Maricela squealed. Chica Linda snorted as if saying, *Serves her right.* Lucky giggled.

"It's not funny!" Maricela cried. In trying to wipe away the dirt, she had made the smudge larger. "Those brutes just ruined my dress. Oh, they're horrible."

"*They're* horrible?" Lucky asked.

Maricela glowered at her. "Are you actually taking their side? You're the granddaughter of a railroad baron. You're supposed to have class."

A voice in Lucky's head told her to stay quiet and let the comment fade like an echo, lest she make an enemy. But another voice, the Prescott voice, couldn't hold back. "Sorry, Maricela, but I guess you're in a *class* all by yourself."

Maricela's face became a cold mask. Even her voice turned icy. "You're new here, so you don't know how things work. But think about this, *Fortuna*"—she leaned real close—"if you're not my friend, then whose friend will you be?" She turned on her heels and huffily stomped back to the schoolhouse.

Lucky sighed. First day, first enemy. How could things get any worse?

She opened her satchel only to remember that the stallion had eaten her entire lunch.

That's how.

At two o'clock, the students grabbed their belongings and scrambled out of the schoolhouse as if it had been set on fire. Shrieks and squeals of glee erupted as kids dashed this way and that, skipping, chasing, and riding to freedom. *Guess everyone has plans*, Lucky thought.

"Good-bye," Miss Flores called, then she began to clean the last lesson from her chalkboard. She glanced over her shoulder at Lucky, who was the only student in the room. "So, Lucky, how was your first day?" Chalk dust drifted off the board.

Lucky shrugged. "Okay, I guess."

Miss Flores half smiled. "Really? It looked a bit rough to me."

Lucky's shoulders fell. "Yeah, it was." Maricela had glared at her all afternoon, and while Abigail and Pru hadn't been outright mean, they hadn't made any further conversation with her. "Someone called me a tenderfoot."

"Oh, that's not such a bad thing. It just means 'newcomer.'"

"They don't like me because I'm not from around here," Lucky said.

Miss Flores set aside the eraser, then sat on the edge of her desk and folded her hands in a thoughtful way. "My first day in Miradero was rough, too. The teacher I'd been hired to replace was named Mr. Barnes. He was as ancient as the canyons." She chuckled. "The kids adored him, mostly because he couldn't hear anything and because he'd take naps at his desk. *Lots* of naps." She wiped chalk dust from her hand. "People in these parts don't like change. It took weeks for them to give me a chance."

"Weeks?" Lucky didn't want to imagine weeks of sitting alone at lunch.

Miss Flores reached across her desk and picked up a yellow flower. "You know, my students often bring these little gifts. Sometimes a flower, sometimes a pear. In the fall they bring me squash or acorns. But it was two long months before the first gift was given. It was a small apple with brown spots and a bruise, but I didn't care because it was the thought that counted. The apple meant that I'd been accepted." She handed the flower to Lucky. "Don't worry; they'll give you a chance. Just be patient. It takes time for people to adjust to new things."

"Thank you," Lucky said, appreciating Miss Flores's kind words. She twirled the flower between her fingers.

"Can I give you a little piece of advice?" Miss Flores asked. Lucky nodded. "Ask your father to take you to the general store. They have some nice, practical clothes. I think it would help. The dress is very pretty, but you might be more comfortable in something less formal."

The advice was spot-on and well intentioned. Lucky said good-bye and headed out the door. She couldn't wait to get back to the house and take off the pink dress. Of all the things she could have worn on the first day of school, it had been the absolute worst choice. "Of course they think I'm a snob," she grumbled to herself. "Thank you very much, Aunt Cora."

Lucky stopped at the corral to check on the stallion. Maybe his day had gone better. Maybe he'd made friends with the other horses.

But there he was, standing alone.

"Sorry, boy, I don't have anything to feed you this time," she said.

Lucky climbed onto the fence and reached out to

the stallion, hoping to coax him over, when a loud voice hollered, "Get away from there, young lady! That horse is dangerous!"

Lucky didn't even look to see who was hollering at her. She'd had enough. Miss Flores was the only nice person in this entire town! The flower fell from her fingers as she ran.

21

Whenever Lucky returned home from Madame
Barrow's Finishing School for Young Ladies, the house
would smell of something lovely, like cinnamon or
chocolate. Mrs. MacFinn would present her with a snack
she'd baked earlier in the day. There'd be a cozy fire in
the parlor, Lucky's favorite place to do her homework.
Sometimes Emma came home with her, and they'd play
dominoes or go to the park to feed the swans.

But there'd be no Emma today. Lucky missed her best
friend more than she could bear. And that is why, when
Aunt Cora asked, "How was your day?" Lucky couldn't
manage a single word. So many emotions washed over
her—anger, frustration, and grief. She stomped loudly up
the stairs.

"Are you hungry?" Cora called. "I walked into town
and got some bread and jam." While that sounded
delicious, especially since she hadn't eaten lunch, Lucky
had something more important to deal with.

As soon as she was in her bedroom, she kicked off
her shoes. Then she grabbed a handful of ruffles and
began to pull up the dress. But it got stuck around her
shoulders, as if it didn't want to come off. "Stupid dress!"

She pulled and yanked, jumped up and down. "Oh, I hate you!" she exclaimed, her voice muffled by layers of silk. "I'm never wearing you again!" With another tug, the dress finally came off. She threw it to the floor, kicked it a few times, then looked up to see that Cora had been in the doorway, witnessing the entire scene.

Standing in her undershirt and bloomers, Lucky felt free for the first time that day. She pointed at the dress. "That was a disaster, by the way. Thank you very much."

Cora put her hands on her hips and frowned. "Look here, young lady, you can take your frustrations out on me, but you're not the only one who's had a terrible day."

Lucky waited for Cora to pick up the dress, to inspect it for stains. To lecture her about hanging it up. But none of that happened. Instead, Cora stepped over the dress, then sat on the edge of Lucky's bed. She wore her usual white blouse and pearls, and her hair was pulled and pinned into a tidy bun. But dark circles loomed beneath Cora's eyes, and she chewed on her lower lip, a habit she often lectured against.

Lucky thought of the famous saying "misery loves company," which means that if you're feeling bad, it often helps to find someone else who is also feeling bad, and then you know you're not alone. Lucky sat next to her aunt. "You had a terrible day? What happened?"

Cora threw her arms into the air. "What *didn't* happen? I went into town only to discover there are no French bakeries. Can you imagine? The lady at the general store had never heard of a croissant or a baguette. And there are no employment agencies, so finding a housekeeper is going to take an excruciatingly long time. Then I discovered that there are no parasols for sale in this town. Because of that nasty goat, I had to mail-order a new one, and it'll take at least a month to get here. Your father hasn't been home all day, so I had to pull apart the shipping crates for firewood. The porcupine came back. He sat on the porch for an entire hour, blocking the door, then he went under the house. I think he lives down there. Between doing the laundry and chasing the world's largest spiders, I haven't had any time to begin my correspondences back home. My friends will think I'm rude if I don't write." She'd spoken so quickly, she was out of breath. "And the hardest part of this move is that I have no one to talk to. I'm not used to being alone all day. I have no…no friends here."

That last statement rang very true for Lucky. "I'm sorry," she said softly. "That does sound like a cruddy day." Lucky was about to launch into her own list of terrible things that had happened, but she decided to wait. Cora seemed to need a moment of silence. So they sat on the bed for a while, Cora catching her breath, Lucky staring at her bare feet and wondering how she could talk Cora into going to the general store to buy pants and cowboy boots.

"There is one piece of good news," Cora said.

"Really?" All sorts of possibilities ran through Lucky's mind. Maybe her aunt would say, *Emma misses you so much she's moving to Miradero.* Or even better, *The railroad's expansion has been canceled and we're going back home.* "What is it?"

Cora's face lit up. "We've been invited to the mayor's house for dinner."

What? This was terrible news. The last thing Lucky wanted to do was to spend time with Maricela. "I'm not going," she said emphatically.

"Of course you're going."

"No, I'm not. Maricela is the meanest girl I have ever met."

Aunt Cora slowly stood and her voice returned to its normal stern tone. "The mayor and his family are important members of this town, and it would be rude to refuse their lovely invitation. We are a family and we *will* go together." Then she pointed at the dress. "That is not how we treat our clothing, Lucky."

While Cora busied herself downstairs, Lucky tucked

the pink dress into the back of her wardrobe, hoping the giant spiders would find it and eat it. Then she put on her bathrobe and stayed in her room, watching out the window for her father. She would appeal to him—maybe fake a stomachache—whatever it took so she didn't have to go to Maricela's house. To pass the time, she tried to write a letter to Emma. But every time she started the first sentence, she crossed it out. Did she really want to tell Emma how terrible everything was? How she'd seen a beautiful horse get captured. How the kids at school thought she was a snob. How her Aunt Cora was driving her crazy. That was not the kind of letter she wanted to write.

Dear Emma,

It's pretty here. The mountains are made of iron oxide so they turn bright-orange when the sun hits them. The sun shines all the time, so I don't need my wool coats or wool socks. On our first day we met a porcupine and a skunk. I wish you could have seen the look on Aunt Cora's face when she realized they'd been living in our house.

There are herds of wild horses that run free in the canyons. They're called mustangs, and on the train ride I saw one of the mustangs get caught. It was terrible! He's the most beautiful horse I've ever seen. A rancher is keeping him in a pen. They want to tame him, which I think isn't very fair. Why can't they let him live in the wild, the way he's supposed to live? I'll keep checking on him, and I'll tell you what happens.

How was your birthday? Did you have fun? Did you like your presents? Is anything interesting happening at school?

Tonight we are going to the mayor's house for dinner. I don't really want to go, but Aunt Cora says I have to. I miss you so much. Please write as soon as you can, and tell me everything!

Your best friend,

Lucky

She folded the paper and set it aside. Oh, how she longed to get a letter from Emma, but Lucky knew that the mail was delivered only a few times a month. Not enough time had passed to get a letter from her best friend.

Jim returned just before twilight, whistling and walking at a happy, brisk pace. *At least someone had a good day,* Lucky thought. She ran downstairs and straight into his arms for a giant bear hug.

"Hi, sweet pea."

"Hi, Dad."

"I love this place," he told her. "It reminds me of those happy years with your mother. I've missed the frontier." Jim's enthusiasm was the wind that blew right through Lucky's cloudy mood. He changed into his waistcoat, adding his favorite pocket watch. Because she'd promised to be brave, Lucky didn't try to get out of the dinner. She put on a blue cotton dress, and they all set out for the mayor's house. Maybe it wouldn't be a terrible time. Maybe she'd misjudged Maricela. She certainly hoped that was the case.

Lucky had been invited to countless dinners during her young life. She'd eaten in the homes of senators, bankers, art dealers, and philanthropists. She'd been served raw oysters, foie gras, and escargot with truffle sauce. Often she'd sat with the other kids at a separate table, so they wouldn't have to endure the boring adult conversations. But dinner at the mayor's house was different because they all sat at the same table. And no one actually spoke to her. The mayor and Jim talked the whole time about the railroad. Cora tried to make polite conversation with Mrs. Gutierrez about the history of the town, but Mrs. Gutierrez seemed interested only in talking about her fine china and her imported linens. She pointed out her antiques as if her possessions were the most important things in the world. And Maricela sat across from Lucky, glaring at her before, during, and after every bite. Lucky didn't really mind that no one was talking to her. It gave her more time to eat the main dish, which was beef stew with spring carrots. Having eaten no lunch or after-school snack, Lucky was famished. Despite Cora's warning glance, she took a second helping of stew *and* a second slice of applesauce cake.

When the meal was over, the adults made their way to the parlor. Maricela motioned for Lucky to follow her up the stairs. Lucky ignored her, but that didn't work, because Maricela grabbed her by the sleeve. "Come on," she urged. "I want to tell you something. *In private.*"

Maricela's bedroom had a four-poster bed with a white ruffled canopy. There were so many pillows, Lucky could barely see the bedspread. Maricela closed the door, then said, "I've decided to give you a second chance to be my best friend." She waited for Lucky's reaction. Was she expecting Lucky to start cheering? Or applauding?

What if I don't want to be your best friend? Lucky considered saying. But instead she said, "Thanks, but I already have a best friend. Her name is Emma."

"Oh really?" Maricela wound a lock of hair around her finger. "And where is Emma?"

"She's back home."

"So you'd rather have a best friend who is all the way on the other side of the world than a best friend here in Miradero?"

"It's not the other side of the world."

Maricela shrugged. "It seems to me that unless Emma moves here, you're going to face a very long year of sitting alone at lunch and not having anyone invite you to parties. Believe me, being my best friend is what you should do."

Why was everyone always telling Lucky what she should do? *Wear this dress. Go to this dinner. Be this person's friend.*

Maricela tucked her pleated skirt under her legs as she sat on the window seat. "But if we're going to be best friends, there are a few rules." She patted the cushion, offering Lucky the space next to her.

Rules? Lucky and Emma didn't have rules. They were best friends because they cared about each other and they loved being together.

Keeping as much distance between them as the window seat allowed, Lucky sat next to the mayor's daughter. Sitting did not mean she was accepting the friendship invitation—it simply meant that she was curious. "What kind of *rules* do you have in mind?"

Maricela raised one eyebrow, as if she were about to reveal an evil scheme. "I tried really hard to be friends with Pru and Abigail, but Pru doesn't like me. She says I'm a snob, as if that's something bad." She rolled her eyes. "So rule number one is, Pru and Abigail aren't our friends."

Lucky frowned. "I don't really have a choice. *They* don't like *me*."

"Excellent. Moving on to rule number two—we don't ride horses. Ever."

Lucky narrowed her eyes. Even though she wasn't allowed to ride, she wanted to challenge Maricela. "Why? Because it's not ladylike?"

"Yes, exactly. It's not ladylike." She paused. "But there's another reason. Riding is what Pru and Abigail do. It's their whole life. But we do other stuff, stuff that takes training and skill."

The poster of *El Circo Dos Grillos* flashed into Lucky's mind—her mother balancing on one leg on her horse's back. "I'm pretty sure horse riding takes a lot of skill."

"Of course it doesn't. *Anyone* can ride a horse. But not everyone can play the piano or speak French. *Comprenez-vous?*" It was bad enough that Maricela was dictating friendship rules, but she was also denying the talent and achievements of Lucky's mother.

"You don't know what you're talking about," Lucky said through clenched teeth.

Maricela's eyes widened.

"Sweetie," Mrs. Gutierrez called from downstairs. "Do come down and entertain us with your lovely playing."

"I'll show you what talent is," Maricela said as she sauntered from her bedroom. She and Lucky joined their parents in the parlor, where Maricela strode up to the piano and curtsied. Her parents applauded. Cora and Jim joined in. Lucky, ignoring her aunt's heated stare, refused to clap.

"What are you going to play, my darling?" asked Mr. Gutierrez.

"I shall play Beethoven's Symphony No. Five," Maricela announced with a flip of her hair. She sat on the piano bench, stretched her fingers, then held them above the keys like stubby snakes ready to attack. And attack they did. The sound that erupted from the piano was so bad, Lucky wanted to plug her ears. Jim coughed, covering a laugh. Even Cora was grimacing. And the "music" went on and on. Sitting in that parlor, enduring the cacophony of notes erupting from the ebony and ivory keys, Lucky squirmed like a worm on a hot rock. Her father was doing his best to hide his amusement, but when they made eye contact, neither could hold back the laughter. Fortunately, the mayor and his wife didn't seem to notice the audience's reaction.

When the ear splitting was finally over, Maricela curtsied again, to her parents' delight.

"Encore! Encore!" they cried.

Cora gave Jim and Lucky her fiercest warning glance. Then she stood. "I think it's time to leave. Thank you so much for your lovely hospitality." She ushered Jim and Lucky to the door before the laughter could begin anew.

"Lucky!" Maricela called, hurrying after her. "I forgot to mention rule number three."

Lucky stopped smiling and stepped away from her father. "What's that?"

Maricela lowered her voice. "You can't hang around with Pru or Abigail."

"I'm *not* following that rule. That's mean."

Maricela crossed her arms and stuck out her chin. "If you don't, then we can't be best friends."

"That's fine by me." Lucky didn't wait for Maricela's reaction. She turned away and hurried to catch up with her dad and aunt.

Well, now she had *zero* new friends.

"What a delightful family," Cora said as they walked up the hill.

"Yes, *delightful*," Jim said.

Expecting Cora to lecture her, Lucky was surprised to hear her aunt say instead, "Ludwig van Beethoven is probably rolling over in his grave after that performance."

"You okay?" Jim reached out and took Lucky's hand. She didn't want to burden him with her troubles. So she just nodded, then let the quiet wrap around them, her hand warming in his.

When they got home, a surprise was waiting on her bed. "Pants!" Lucky cried after untying the cord and opening the brown paper package.

Jim stuck his head into her room. "Yup, got them at the general store today. I figured it would help you feel more at home here."

She hugged him. "Oh, thank you, Dad!"

"I got a pair for your aunt, too." He held a finger in the air. "Wait for it…"

From Cora's room came the sound of crinkling paper and then a gasp. "Pants? Never!"

Lucky and her dad shared a quiet chuckle. But Lucky remembered the sad look on her aunt's face when she'd mentioned that she had no friends. Maybe tomorrow would be a better day for them both.

22

Another night had arrived and the stallion was still surrounded by fence. Being penned in was nearly driving him mad. Staying in one place went against all his instincts. To wander, to roam, and to seek was the natural inclination of his kind. Yet all he could do in this dreadful place was to pace, around and around. A deep groove formed in the dirt beneath his hooves.

He fretted for his herd's safety. How would they manage without him? He remembered when a mountain lion had tried to take one of the foals. Only a few days old, the foal had been lying next to its mother, sleeping. The lion had crept silently, as lions do, camouflaged by the brown grasses of late summer. But the crisp snap of a single twig had alerted the stallion. He charged at the lion, face-to-face. The great cat growled and slashed with its claws. The stallion reared and stomped, his hoof landing on the lion's paw, causing just enough pain to make it turn and flee.

He remembered another time when a pair of foals, twins, had been playing on the ridge. They'd wandered away from the herd and when he found them, one stood dangerously close to a cliff. The stallion slipped between the foal and the cliff, his hooves teetering on the edge. But he managed to push the foal back to safety.

That's how a herd works. They watch out for one another. They look after the young ones and the old ones. But how would they fare without him?

He paced, around and around, the groove deepening.

23

The next morning, Lucky awoke to sparrow song
and a cloudless blue sky. It was a lovely start to the day,
but Lucky didn't want to wake up. While she'd dealt
with nerves on her first day of school, her stomach felt
even tighter on this, her second day. So many things had
already gone wrong. If only she could erase it all and
start over.

She sat up. That's exactly what she'd do. She'd
pretend that yesterday never happened and today was
the beginning. She'd explain things to Pru and Abigail.
If they understood that she actually liked horses, they'd
surely give her a second chance. She'd even be nice to
the mayor's obnoxious daughter. That would be tough,
but if Lucky was expecting a second chance, then she
should grant one to Maricela, too. She had a plan, which
was better than losing hope. *Prescotts do not run from
challenges.*

There were no pancakes that morning, because
Cora had been distracted by an important project. She'd
borrowed Lucky's art supplies and was seated at the
kitchen table, creating some posters. "What are those?"
Lucky asked.

"I've had a brilliant idea. I'm going to bring culture to the frontier," Cora said as she dipped a paintbrush into paint. "There are no art or history museums in this town. They don't even have an opera house. We must change that, and I shall be the one to lead the revolution."

Attention, Ladies of Miradero!

You are most welcome to attend
the first meeting of the

Miradero Ladies' Social Betterment Society

The Prescott Home,
tonight at 6:00 pm

Refreshments will be served.

"That looks good," Lucky told her. Cora smiled at her work. She was so focused on her lettering, she didn't notice that Lucky was wearing the new pair of pants. It was nice to start the day without a battle over clothing choices. "Don't forget your lunch," Cora said as she added more paint to her brush.

"Thanks." Lucky grabbed her lunch bag and an extra apple. She glanced back at Cora, and her stomach suddenly felt better. Lucky wasn't going to give up, and it looked as if Cora felt the same way. Maybe things would work out. They were Prescotts, after all.

Jim was sitting on the front porch steps, enjoying his morning coffee, a platter of toast at his side. Lucky sat beside him and helped herself to a slice. "Isn't this country beautiful?" he said, gazing toward the mountains.

"Uh-huh," she said while chewing.

He smiled, noticing her clothes. "Hey, you look like you've lived in Miradero all your life. Want me to walk you to school?"

It was a tempting offer, but with Maricela mad at her, and Pru and Abigail thinking she was a horse-hating snob, she didn't want her father to see the other kids shun her. "I'm okay on my own," she said.

"Gotcha."

After another piece of toast and a kiss good-bye,

Lucky ran down the driveway. "Don't run!" Cora's voice called after her. "You might fall and hurt yourself!" What was the deal? Did she have eyes in the back of her head? Lucky appeased her aunt, but only until she was out of view; then she started running again, all the way to the corral, hoping to find the stallion so she could feed him the extra apple. She also hoped no one would be there so she wouldn't get yelled at again. She ran fast so she'd have as much time as possible before the school bell rang. How nice it was to run in pants. When she darted around the corner of the barn, she skidded to a stop. Her heart sank.

The stallion wasn't alone.

A tall man with a black beard stood inside the corral. He pushed his tan cowboy hat from his eyes. The stallion moved around the man, keeping his distance. A few ranch hands leaned against the fence, watching. Lucky approached quietly. Fortunately, everyone was distracted and took no notice of her. Except for a boy with messy brown hair.

"Hi." He walked up to Lucky and smiled. "I'm Turo. You must be the new girl."

"I'm Lucky," she told him.

"Yeah, I heard you'd arrived." He seemed a bit older than she was. "I wasn't in school yesterday," he explained, patting his leather apron. "I'm apprenticing at the blacksmith's shop and when we get extra work, I'm allowed to miss school."

"Who's that man, and what's he doing?" Lucky asked, pointing into the corral.

"That's Mr. Granger. He owns this ranch. Come on. We can go watch." He motioned for Lucky to follow, and they found a spot next to the fence, away from the ranch hands.

Lucky remembered that Pru's last name was Granger. That man must be her father.

Turo was tall enough to see over the fence, but Lucky had to step on the lower board to get a better view. "Mr. Granger is trying to wear the horse down," Turo explained. "So he won't fight so much. But that horse just won't tire. Look at him."

The stallion didn't seem tired. His nostrils flared, and he glared at his captor. The morning sun gleamed off Mr. Granger's silver belt buckle and highlighted the golden tones in the stallion's coat.

"His color is so pretty," Lucky said.

"Yeah, that's called buckskin. It's the same color as tanned deerskin."

The stallion stopped trotting as one of the ranch hands climbed over the fence and handed something to Mr. Granger. The stallion neighed at the ranch hand, who, with a look of terror, jumped back quickly over the fence to safety.

"Now what's he doing?" Lucky asked.

"He's going to try to introduce a halter and a lead." Turo noticed Lucky's questioning look. "A halter is the piece that goes over the horse's face. And the lead is the rope that hangs down from the halter so you can lead the horse where you want to go."

"It's okay, boy," Mr. Granger said, trying to get close. "It's okay. I'm not gonna hurt you. Come on now." An odd dance followed. As Mr. Granger stepped closer, the stallion stepped away. If Mr. Granger sped up, the stallion sped up. "Walt, Henry, get in here and help me."

Walt and Henry didn't look like they wanted to help. They pushed each other, trying to make the other go first.

"Get in here!" Mr. Granger repeated. The two ranch hands climbed over the fence. But the minute their feet touched down, the stallion went berserk, whinnying and rearing. "Watch out!" The front legs came crashing down, barely missing Walt, who scrambled back over the fence. Then, after a swift buck, the back legs came down, breaking a piece of the fence next to Henry, who was already halfway over. The stallion, eyes burning with rage, turned his attention to Mr. Granger. He neighed again and shot forward. Mr. Granger dove over the fence like a trapeze artist. Lucky gasped as he landed, facedown, in the grass.

The stallion snorted a few times, which sounded a bit like laughter. While Lucky didn't want anyone to get hurt, she felt a surge of pride for the stallion. He was defending himself. Good for him!

"Mr. Granger, sir? You okay?" Walt asked, leaning over his boss. He reached out a hand but Mr. Granger whacked it away.

The stallion snorted. Then, as if Mr. Granger were nothing more than a pesky fly, the stallion swished his tail and turned away. It was an opportunity not to be missed. With the stallion's gaze elsewhere, Mr. Granger grabbed a handful of mane and swung quickly onto the stallion's back, taking the creature completely by surprise. Lucky gasped. For a brief moment, Mr. Granger was sitting on the stallion's back, grinning from ear to ear.

Then the stallion bucked and, once again, Mr. Granger soared over the fence and landed in the grass.

"If Mr. Granger can't ride that mustang, no one can," Turo whispered in Lucky's ear.

Mr. Granger took off his red bandana and wiped his glistening forehead. "More time is all I need. More time and he'll break. They all do." The stallion stomped around the corral, tossing his mane defiantly.

Mr. Granger got to his feet, turned and pointed at Turo and Lucky. "You kids stay away from that mustang. He'll bite you if you get too close!" Then Mr. Granger and his ranch hands walked into the barn.

"I'd better get back to work," Turo said. "See you later." He moseyed across the street to the blacksmith's shop, leaving Lucky alone with the stallion.

Oh, how she wished she could set him free!

"Hello, boy," she said.

The stallion's proud stance melted, as if he also realized that they were alone. Suddenly, she could see his fatigue. His shoulders sagged. Droplets fell from his nostrils as he panted. He'd been putting on a show for Mr. Granger, hiding his exhaustion. But with Lucky, he didn't hide the truth. She reached out her hand. "Here you go, boy, here's a treat." He took the apple, then she gave him the one from her lunch bag, too. She touched his cheek. His face was warm and damp with sweat. "I'm sorry," she told him. "I'm sorry for everything that's happening to you."

Miss Flores had said it took time for people to adjust to new things. Lucky realized that animals needed time, too. Eventually, the stallion would be broken. The wild spirit would be tamed out of him. But where would that wild spirit go? Would it drift away, over the mountains, to a place where wildness was allowed and celebrated?

If only such a place existed.

Bong. Bong.

With all her heart she wanted to stay with him, to tell him that everything would be all right. But she had a plan for a new beginning. And the new beginning was calling.

24

The men were gone. The girl was gone. Alone once
again, the stallion finally allowed his legs to buckle. He
sank to the ground. Lying on the dirt was a welcome
relief. Over the past few days he'd done his best to hold
his head high, to defy the men in every way possible. To
not eat their food. To not show them weakness. But he
desperately needed to rest.

Even a wild horse needed rest.

He allowed his eyes to close, but kept his ears alert,
picking up the sounds of the tamed horses out in the
pasture. But there were no sounds of his herd thundering
across the wilderness. They were smart to stay away
from this place. Far from the men with the ropes.

He thought about the girl, the one with the sweet
treats. Why did she keep coming to see him? She was
smaller than the others, and different. She spoke to him
without force. She looked at him without aggression.

He trusted her.

The tall man was back. The stallion bolted to his feet,
his eyes blazing.

"Okay, horse, let's try this again."

25

While erasing a drawing simply requires a good
eraser and some muscle, erasing an entire day is another
matter entirely. Lucky, being kindhearted and genuine in
her intent, might have had success at starting anew with
the students at school, were it not for Maricela.

Maricela, still angry with Lucky for not agreeing to
her friendship rules, was apparently on a mission. She
spent that entire school day whispering in ears and
pointing as Lucky passed by. Lucky could only imagine
the horrid lies coming out of Maricela's mouth. *That
new girl thinks she's better than everyone else. That new
girl hates horses. That new girl says terrible things about
all of you.* With a fake sweet smile, Maricela spread her
meanness like icing on a cake, only this cake was sour
and full of lies.

Lucky tried her best to focus on the schoolwork and
to listen to Miss Flores's lessons. It was killing her how
much fun Pru and Abigail seemed to have together,
brushing their horses at lunch and laughing. But each
time she tried to approach them, Maricela got there
first, to fill their heads with more lies. Lucky tried to stay
positive, but it was getting more and more difficult.

At the end of the day, she didn't wait around for Miss Flores to offer advice. It was too painful to have her rejection acknowledged. So she scooted out, just behind the rest of the students. She'd go see the stallion again. Maybe he was feeling better. But just before she reached the blacksmith's shop, she heard two familiar voices.

"Can you please fix the strap on my stirrup, Turo? It came loose again." That was Pru's voice.

"Sure." That was Turo's.

Lucky stopped walking. The voices drifted from the other side of the building. She pressed against the wall. Yes, she was eavesdropping, but only to gather more information in her attempt to make new friends. She peeked around the corner. Yes, she was spying, but *stop telling me what to do, Aunt Cora*, she said to the voice in her head. *I don't care if it's rude; I need to see what's going on.*

Pru sat on Chica Linda while Turo worked on the strap. While waiting, Abigail was weaving a ribbon into Boomerang's mane.

"We're going to look for arrowheads tomorrow, so I need the strap good and tight," Pru told Turo. "Abigail, what are you doing?"

"I'm putting a ribbon on Boomerang, like the one Lucky wears."

Lucky reached back and felt her ribbon. She smiled. Abigail had noticed.

"I met Lucky this morning," Turo said. "She seems nice. Are you friends?"

Lucky leaned farther, hoping to see smiles on their faces. But Pru frowned. "Maricela is her friend."

"I don't think that's true," Abigail said. "Maricela wasn't talking to her at school today. And she was saying all sorts of mean things."

"Maricela always says mean things," Turo pointed out. "Why don't you invite Lucky to go look for arrowheads?"

"That's a good idea." Abigail kissed Boomerang's cheek. Then she climbed into her saddle. "Maybe Lucky isn't as bad as Maricela says."

"You've forgotten that she doesn't ride," Pru said. "She's a *lady*." Lucky cringed. She was really starting to hate that word.

"Whatcha doin'?"

Lucky whipped around. Snips, Abigail's little brother, stood just a few feet away, looking up at her with a goofy grin. He was a cute kid, with a mop of dark-red hair and freckles all over his face.

"Wanna see my new bug?" He opened his little pudgy hand to reveal a shiny black beetle.

"That's very nice," Lucky whispered. She peeked around the side of the blacksmith shop to make sure Pru and Abigail hadn't caught her spying. But they were riding away together, and Turo had gone back inside.

Snips tugged happily on Lucky's pant leg. "Wanna play with me?"

Hanging out with a six-year-old wouldn't normally be on Lucky's to-do list, but she didn't want to hurt his feelings. "I've got an…appointment," she said, intending to visit the stallion. "How come you didn't ride home with your sister?"

He stuck the beetle on his head and giggled as it climbed through his hair. "She's goin' somewhere with Pru. Like always." Just as he reached up to reclaim his prize, the beetle wisely flew away. Snips picked up a rock and threw it at a tree. "Where's *your* horse?"

"I don't have one."

"You don't got a horse?" He threw another rock, then ran around a large barrel that was filled with water. "I got a horse." He puffed out his chest. "His name is Señor Carrots. I ride him all by myself."

"Well, that's nice," Lucky said, starting across the road toward the corral. "See you later."

Snips didn't take the hint. He stumbled after her, his

little legs working hard to keep up. "You can come ride Señor Carrots anytime you want."

Lucky stopped walking. Snips bumped right into her. "Did you just say I can ride your horse?" she asked.

"Yup. That's what I said."

This was an interesting turn of events. Lucky knew that in order to fit in with the local kids, she'd have to learn to ride. And there was no doubt Aunt Cora wouldn't allow such an activity. Therefore, finding someone to give her riding lessons would require stealth. Had opportunity appeared in the form of a hyper, redheaded six-year-old? Surely if Snips could ride Señor Carrots, then Lucky could ride him. He had to be a very gentle horse to be given to such a young boy.

"Can I try right now?"

"Yay!" Snips jumped up and down. "Oh goody, I can't wait for you to meet Señor Carrots." He twirled around in a little happy dance.

Okay, this was really happening. Lucky was in cahoots with a kid barely old enough to tie his own shoes. But a professional riding lesson would cost money and would be difficult to find without Cora's permission. Lucky had to grab her chance while it wiggled in front of her, freckles and all. If she could learn on Señor Carrots, then she could show her father what a great rider she was, and he could help her change Cora's mind.

But she still wanted to see the stallion. She'd go as soon as the lesson was over.

The Stone family's house was white with blue shutters. It had a big wraparound front porch and a pretty backyard with a shade tree, a rope swing, and a little garden shed.

"How come you call him Señor Carrots?" Lucky asked, even though she'd guessed the answer.

"Because it's his favorite food." They stood in the backyard. Snips cupped his hands around his mouth and hollered, "Señor Carrots!" This struck Lucky as odd because, first of all, there was no horse standing in the small, fenced backyard. Second, there was no barn, either. The only place Señor Carrots could be was behind the shed, but that was way too small to hide an entire horse. Snips stomped over to the shed, looked behind it, and said, "I see you, Señor Carrots."

A braying sound followed. Then a gray head appeared, followed by a gray body. It was the smallest horse Lucky had ever seen. "Is that a baby?" she asked with surprise.

"He's not a baby, silly. He's a donkey!" As if in agreement, Señor Carrots made a loud *hee-haw* sound.

This was not at all what Lucky had expected. She'd envisioned Señor Carrots as a dashing steed. He'd bow when he met her, allowing her to climb easily into the saddle. After a few minutes of riding, she'd stand on the saddle and balance on one leg, just like her mother. Then she'd hold that pose right down the main street and everyone would come out of the shops and applaud. Even Cora would be so overwhelmed with awe, she'd say, "I'm so proud. Prescott proud!" And there'd be no way Cora could refuse Lucky a horse of her own.

But no dashing steed awaited Lucky. Señor Carrots was a funny-looking creature. His mane was short and stuck straight up, like perfectly trimmed grass. And he was swaybacked, with a very round belly. He began to chew on the suspenders that held Snips's shorts. "Stop it," Snips said, pushing him away. "Okay, I'll show you how to ride him." Snips went into the gardening shed and came out with a bucket and a couple of carrots. He turned the bucket over, set it on the ground, then climbed onto it. Holding out a carrot, he whistled for his donkey, who hurried over, grabbed the carrot with his buck teeth, then knocked Snips over. Snips tumbled off the bucket, landing in the grass. After a frustrated groan, Snips got to his feet and repeated the process, but this time, when the second carrot was snatched, Snips grabbed the donkey's mane. "Come on, let me ride you," Snips whined. But the donkey pulled away, and once again Snips landed in the grass. "Ooh, you bad donkey." Señor Carrots brayed again and again. Was he laughing? Then, in a short-stepped and jerky way, he trotted right past Lucky. When she turned around, she realized she'd left the gate open.

"Uh-oh," she said as the donkey headed out of the yard. "Señor Carrots!" At the sound of his name, the donkey picked up speed.

As Lucky chased the donkey up the street, the scene from the train came to mind—the stallion galloping, the two *mesteñeros* in pursuit, ropes swinging. If they could catch the wildest, fastest horse in these parts, then surely catching a squat, ill-behaved donkey couldn't be too hard. Fortunately, some flowers sprouting in front of Town Hall caught the donkey's attention and he stopped to graze. "Gotcha," Lucky declared as she wrapped her arms around his neck.

The donkey wiggled free, then bumped Lucky aside, knocking her to the ground. "Ow," she said as she landed on her rump in the dirt. The donkey brayed, exposing his buck teeth. Was he going to bite her? There wasn't enough time to scramble away. Lucky quickly covered her face with her hands, expecting a sharp pain, but what she got instead was a lick.

"Señor Carrots likes you," Snips said. "He doesn't like anyone. How come he likes you?"

Señor Carrots pushed Snips out of the way, then licked Lucky's face again. She laughed.

"Lucky!"

Lucky looked up. Cora stood over her, holding a large basket that was brimming with groceries.

Uh-oh.

26

"What in the world do you think you're doing
sitting in the dirt?"

"Nothing," Lucky grumbled.

Señor Carrots turned his attention to the basket,
which Cora yanked away. "Shoo, shoo," she told the
donkey. "Young man, is this your creature? You shouldn't
allow him to roam the streets. Have you no regard for
public safety? He tried to take a bite out of me."

"Sorry, ma'am," Snips said. "Señor Carrots bites
everyone. Even me. But he loves Lucky." Then he smiled
at Lucky. "You still wanna ride him?"

"What's this?" Cora pursed her lips. "*Ride* him?"

Lucky stood and wiped dirt off her backside. "Don't
worry, Aunt Cora. I wouldn't ride this donkey. He's way
too small."

"That, *and* you're not allowed to ride." Cora wrapped
her arms around the basket as the donkey tried to steal
a head of lettuce. "Let's go. I need your help setting up
for tonight's meeting of the Miradero Ladies' Social
Betterment Society."

"Bye, Lucky!" Snips called. Lucky waved. Snips gave
the donkey a shove. The donkey gave Snips a head butt.

Then the two of them headed home. So much for a riding lesson.

To Lucky's surprise, Cora didn't launch into a lecture about breaking rules or safety or any such thing. Her cheeks pink with excitement and her blue eyes twinkling, she was focused on the evening's event. Her smile made Lucky feel happy *and* sad at the same time. Both her father and her aunt seemed to be finding their places in Miradero, and here was Lucky, with only a six-year-old, a donkey, and a captive mustang to call her friends. "You can help me set up for the meeting, can't you? You don't have other plans, do you?"

Other plans? Lucky fidgeted. Yes, she had other plans. She wanted to go see the stallion, but how could she tell her aunt that she'd befriended a wild horse? Cora would never understand. "Sure, I can help." She took the basket from her aunt's arms and they started walking home. *I'll go see him later*, Lucky promised herself.

Lucky helped dust and sweep the living room. She also picked thistles and dandelions and arranged them in a vase. Cora had bought two dozen cookies with dollops of raspberry jam in the center. She set them on a platter. Because Jim was working late, Cora and Lucky ate dinner at five o'clock so the dishes could be done before the six o'clock meeting.

"What's this?" Lucky asked, staring at a bowl of beans and meat.

"It's called chili," Cora told her. "According to the man at the general store, it's a specialty around here."

Lucky took a bite. It was spicy, but good. She ate a bit more, but was surprised to find she didn't have much of an appetite.

"Why aren't you eating?"

"I'm not hungry."

"If you don't eat, you'll get sick." Cora set her spoon down. "You're not sick, are you?" She reached across the table and set her palm on Lucky's forehead.

Lucky sighed. "I'm not sick." She stirred the chili round and round the bowl.

"Then what's wrong?"

She had to say it. She had to be brave and face her aunt. "Aunt Cora, if I'm going to fit in around here, I need to learn how to ride."

Cora wagged a finger at Lucky. "That is *not* happening."

Frustration welled, readying for its escape. "But everyone rides, Aunt Cora. Even Snips, and he's only six years old."

"I said no. It's not appropriate." Cora continued eating the chili.

"You don't understand. Horses like me. They do. I don't know how to explain it, but…" Her frustration reached a boiling point and burst out, like steam in a kettle. "This is totally unfair!" She pushed her food aside. "We're not in the city anymore, so who cares about being *appropriate*? My mom rode horses, so why can't I? I bet Dad will let me!"

Cora dropped her spoon. A bit of chili splattered onto the tablecloth. "I am your aunt and I'm telling you *no*. Do not argue with me, young lady. Riding horses is dangerous. End of discussion."

There they were, once again, face-to-face, the stubborn Prescotts. Lucky pushed back her chair and stomped toward the front door.

"Where are you going?"

"I'm going for a walk!"

"But, Lucky, my guests will be arriving soon. They'll want to meet you. I need your help serving the cookies and coffee."

Lucky pretended she didn't hear her aunt's pleas. The door slammed behind her. She knew she was being rude, but she had a right to be angry. Moving to the frontier and not riding horses was like moving to a tropical island and not swimming. Aunt Cora was being ridiculous!

She ran down the hill. The setting sun had lit the surrounding mountains on fire. A red-tailed hawk flew overhead, and a dog barked in the distance. A pair of round eyes blinked at her from atop Mr. Granger's barn. It was an old owl, readying himself for the twilight hunt. Since it was dinnertime, the ranch hands were in their bunkhouse, lamplight glowing in the windows. From inside came the sounds of utensils scraping plates and laughter as a meal was shared. Mr. Granger's horses were in their barn, closed up for the night.

But in the corral, the stallion stood, his head hanging, his eyes closed. Was he asleep? Lucky tiptoed, not wanting to wake him. But when she reached the fence his eyes popped open, and he turned toward her. "Hello," she whispered. There was sadness in his eyes. She could feel it, as if someone had broken her own heart.

His trough was full of oats, untouched. Why wasn't he eating?

He's stubborn, she realized. He was having a standoff with Mr. Granger, just as she'd had with Cora. Even though Mr. Granger had warned no one to get near, Lucky climbed over the fence and dropped gracefully to the dirt. The stallion's head rose. She scooped the oats into her hands and held them out—an offering, for what more could she do for him than to coax him to eat? "If you don't eat, you'll get sick," she said. She took a step toward him.

"You shouldn't approach a horse like that."

Startled, Lucky dropped the oats. Pru stood outside the fence. Lucky gulped. She was in huge trouble. Surely Pru would go tell her father that the city girl had been trespassing.

"I was just—"

"Yeah, I can see you're trying to feed him. But you're walking toward him from the front. Horses can't see well directly ahead. You should always come up to them from the side. That makes them less nervous."

"Uh, okay." Lucky didn't tell Pru that she and the stallion had already met. She scooped more oats and tried again. He set his muzzle into her palms and ate.

"That's impressive," Pru said, leaning on the fence. "Dad says he's been refusing most of the food. He's the wildest horse ever caught."

Lucky knew why he was refusing. He didn't like Mr. Granger or this place, but he clearly liked her. She grabbed more oats and coaxed the stallion toward the trough until he stuck his nose in and ate.

"Better not let my dad catch you in there," Pru said.

She was right. Lucky climbed back outside the fence. "You're not going to tell?"

"Why would I tell?" Pru gave her a long, measuring look. "Who knew a city girl like you could tame a wild horse? I'm impressed."

"How come your dad is keeping him? Why won't he let him go?" Lucky asked.

"My dad makes his living taming horses. He thinks this stallion will bring in more money than any other horse he's ever broken. He's really special." Pru stuck her hands into her pockets and looked at Lucky. "You seem like a natural with horses. I know you don't ride, but tomorrow Abigail and I are..." She hesitated.

Was Pru going to invite Lucky along? This was a hugely important moment! Lucky waited, fingers crossed behind her back.

Pru kicked a small rock. "Never mind. I gotta go." She walked away, her braid swaying. Lucky's shoulders sagged. She leaned against the fence. *I'm not what you think I am.*

Something bumped against her shoulder. The stallion put his face right up to hers. His breath was warm. He nudged her again.

"Hello, fellow." Lucky pressed her face against his neck. She could feel his heart beating. His musky scent filled her nostrils. It was a mixture of grass and dirt. It made her feel peaceful.

Why did that horse smell feel like home?

"We have so much in common," she told him. "We're both outcasts." She placed her hands on his cheeks and kissed his muzzle. And he let her.

"I'm gonna figure this out, for both of us. I promise."

27

Jim was sitting on the porch when Lucky returned, his legs stretched out and resting on the railing. "Where ya been, sweet pea?"

"Just taking a walk."

"Nice night for a walk. Saw some gorgeous country today. We rode deep into the canyons, down to the river." His smile was big and authentic. He clearly loved everything about Miradero.

"That's nice," Lucky mumbled, only half listening. She dreaded going inside, for she knew she owed her aunt an apology. It was awfully quiet in there—no china tinkling, no conversations. "Did all the guests leave already?"

"I guess so. I just got home a few minutes ago. These cookies are delicious; you want one?" He grabbed the platter of jam cookies. Only three were missing. Why hadn't the guests eaten more?

"Where's Aunt Cora?"

"In her room. She seemed upset about something, so I decided to give her a little space. You know how your aunt gets."

Lucky suspected she was the cause. She made her

way upstairs, took a deep breath, then knocked on her aunt's bedroom door. "Aunt Cora?" There was no answer, so she opened the door. Cora was on the bed, lying on her side, facing the wall. "Are you awake? I'm sorry I got mad at you." Cora didn't say anything. Only sniffled. Lucky stepped in. "Are you crying? Is it because of me?"

"It's not you, Lucky. It's…it's…no one came to my meeting." She sat up and a few tears rolled down her cheeks. Lucky had never seen her aunt cry. *Always keep a stiff upper lip* was one of Cora's favorite sayings. *Tears don't change things; they only make you blotchy* was another.

Cora grabbed a handkerchief and dabbed at her eyes. "What else can I do?" she said. "I've failed. I tried to make friends with Mrs. Gutierrez, but she doesn't share the same interests that I have. And no one in this town wants to talk about art or culture. No one wants to be a part of the Ladies' Social Betterment Society." She blew her nose. "No one wants to be my friend."

Lucky sat next to her aunt. On countless occasions she'd felt that she couldn't relate to Cora, that they had nothing in common other than the Prescott name. But as it turned out, they now shared a common ache.

One of Cora's trunks lay open on the floor. "Are you packing? Are you going to leave?"

Cora turned away as if ashamed. "I know I always say that Prescotts never run from a challenge, but I tried. I really, really tried. I'm not cut out for this place." She stood and walked to the window. "We aren't meant to live in the wilderness, Lucky. We need a more civilized life." She turned and held up her hands. "Look at me. I have calluses and scrapes and bruises on my arms. And look at you. You're wearing *pants*, you have dirt on your face, and you smell like a horse."

Lucky didn't care how she looked or smelled, but she did care how she felt.

Lonely.

"I think we should both leave," Cora said.

"But that would be giving up," Lucky said with surprise. "You *never* give up."

"It's not giving up if we leave. We would simply be making the very best decision in difficult circumstances."

The idea of going home drifted over Lucky like a cool breeze on a hot day. Wouldn't it be a relief to go back to the city? Wouldn't Emma be surprised? Lucky would even be happy to see Madame Barrow again. She imagined the reunion with all the other students, the scones and tea, the new books from Emma's father, parties on the weekend, and Mr. MacFinn's stories about

Scotland and Mrs. MacFinn's cozy dinners. It sounded wonderful.

Except for the fact that her dad wouldn't be there.

"Hey, you two, what's going on up here?" Jim stepped into the room. He noticed the trunks, and a pained expression clouded his face. "Cora? What's all this?"

"Dad, Aunt Cora wants to go back home."

"Yes, and I want to take Lucky with me."

"I'm not sure what to do," Lucky said.

With a heavy sigh, Jim leaned against the doorframe. "I've been so caught up in my work, I haven't helped you two settle in. I'm sorry about that. The last thing I want is for either of you to be unhappy. Of course, I want you to stay, but…" He rubbed the back of his neck. "But if you decide to go back to the city, then I'll understand. But please, think about it. Give it some time. I'll be leaving in the morning to dynamite Filbert Canyon. When I get back, you can tell me what you've decided."

That seemed fair. It was a decision that would not come easily, and Lucky did want time to think about it. She and Cora agreed. Jim managed a sad smile, then walked away, his footsteps heavy and slow.

Tucked in bed that night, Lucky pulled the quilt all the way up to her chin. The fabric still smelled like her old home. She picked up her favorite photo. Her mother had left her village and had moved to a new place, had made new friends, and had thrived in this frontier world. Lucky had always wondered how she was like her mother, and maybe it was time to accept the truth. Other than the way she looked, the color of her skin and hair, perhaps she was nothing like her mom. Perhaps she wasn't brave enough to face this new life.

Lucky had been given the gift of choice—to leave or to stay. Her fate was now in her own hands. But the stallion was still locked up. He had no choice.

And that seemed more unfair than anything else in the world.

28

The stallion had a dream. He was galloping across a meadow with his herd.

Galloping.

Galloping.

The wind on his face. The earth beneath his hooves.

He wanted to stay in that dream forever.

Part Four

29

A familiar dream visited Lucky that night. The audience sat in hushed anticipation as Cowgirl Betty and Shadow stepped out of the wings. Lucky wiggled in her seat, trying to get the best view possible. But she didn't need to worry about peeking around her grandfather's large head, because when Betty held out her hand, Lucky found herself standing on the opera house stage, the ring of fire burning bright. "What am I doing here?" Lucky asked.

Betty smiled. "You're gonna show everyone what you're made of." She set a cowboy hat on Lucky's head, and suddenly Lucky was seated in Shadow's saddle. Betty led Shadow to the edge of the stage. She handed the reins to Lucky. Shadow turned to face the fire, waiting for Lucky to give the command.

"Don't do it! It's too dangerous!" Aunt Cora hollered from the box seat.

Shadow's muscles stiffened as he prepared for the jump. But something didn't feel right. Lucky didn't want to jump. This hadn't been her choice. Her body began to tremble. "No," she said, tugging on the reins, trying to pull Shadow away. "Please, no," she said again as he bolted forward. "I don't want to do this! I'm not ready."

The ring of fire came closer and closer. The air grew hotter and hotter. With a thrust, Shadow lifted off the ground and…

…Lucky bolted upright. Her eyes flew open. She was awake, in her bed, covered in sweat.

"I really *hate* that dream," she grumbled.

Except for her ragged breathing, all was quiet in the house. Then the front door thumped. Lucky hurried to the window. Though the sun had not yet risen, Jim was already on his way to work. He was going to begin dynamiting today, so he was getting an extra-early start.

Last night's conversation replayed in Lucky's mind. Would she go with Aunt Cora or stay with her father? It was an agonizing choice and she was no closer to a resolution than she'd been before falling sleep. But she had made *one* decision.

After dressing in her new pants and a white shirt with a pretty red embroidered trim, she braided her hair and added a ribbon. She tiptoed past Cora's room, though she probably could have walked normally since Cora was snoring so loudly. Fighting the urge to run, she quietly slipped down the stairs and out the front door, closing it without a thump.

Then she took off.

Lucky's one and only decision was about the stallion. She was going to plead with Mr. Granger to set him free. And if Mr. Granger refused because he needed to earn his living, then she'd borrow money from her father or sell all her belongings, whatever it took to buy the stallion from him. Then she'd set him free.

The first rays of morning peeked over the tabletop mountains. A red-tailed hawk swooped overhead. A squirrel scurried up a tree as Lucky ran past. There were no signs of townspeople. Was it too early to knock on Mr. Granger's door?

Lucky ran past Town Hall, then took a sharp left. Just as she reached the Grangers' barn, she heard voices. She skidded to a stop as Pru and Abigail led Chica Linda and Boomerang out of the barn. They were dressed in britches and boots. A small shovel peeked out of Pru's saddlebag. It was certainly an early hour for a ride, but Lucky remembered that the girls were going on a search for arrowheads. Maybe early morning was best for such an adventure before the noon sun heated the desert soil. Not wanting to face another rejection, Lucky darted behind a stack of hay bales. Her choice tugged at her again. Staying in Miradero meant she'd have to learn to ride, and she'd need to work hard to earn Pru and

Abigail's trust. Leaving would mean she wouldn't have to worry about any of that.

Pru stepped into the stirrup, then swung her leg and sat in her saddle. "Come on, Abigail, let's get going."

The girls were going on an adventure without her, and that's just the way it was. Lucky pushed aside her hurt feelings. The focus this morning was the stallion. He was more important than her social life. She'd come to save him.

"Don't you think we should check with your parents before leaving?" Abigail asked as she adjusted her horse's saddle.

"My parents aren't here," Pru said. "Mr. Prescott needed extra help with a special project, so Dad and all the ranch hands are helping with the railroad today. And Mom is in Winslow visiting relatives. Besides, I told Dad last night that we were going to look for arrowheads, and he said to have fun. And you already told your parents that you were riding with me."

"But I thought Filbert Canyon was off-limits," Abigail said.

"Why would it be off-limits? That's where Walt found all his arrowheads. I'm so excited! I'm gonna start a collection."

"Yeah, okay." Abigail didn't sound very excited. She

grabbed the saddle horn and pulled herself up. "You sure it's not too dangerous out there? You know I don't like those steep canyon trails."

"We'll be fine. Filbert Canyon is a blast!" Pru gave Chica Linda a gentle kick. "Come on, girl, let's ride!" Chica Linda took off with Boomerang at her heels.

Lucky groaned. How could she negotiate the stallion's freedom if Mr. Granger wasn't home?

But something more urgent pulled at Lucky, something Abigail had said. *I thought Filbert Canyon was off-limits.* Why did that name seem familiar? Her father's face came to mind, as he stood in Aunt Cora's room, asking Cora and Lucky to take their time in making a decision. *Gone tomorrow. Dynamiting Filbert Canyon.*

"Wait," Lucky said, darting out from behind the bales. "Wait!" she screamed, her hands waving wildly. But the girls were already out of earshot. They were heading in the opposite direction of town, straight toward the mountains. Straight into danger.

Lucky darted into the barn, but no one was there. She pounded on the bunkhouse door. Pru had said all the ranch hands were helping with the railroad today, but maybe someone was left behind. The door wasn't locked, so Lucky burst inside. "Hello? I need help!" A deck of cards sat on a long table. The bunks were all made, the wool blankets folded. The kitchen was tidy, the metal cups lined up in a perfect row. No one was there.

Lucky ran back outside. The blacksmith's shop was empty, too. She strained her eyes against the rising sun. The girls were still visible, but smaller now. It would take forever to run back to town, and soon the girls would be out of sight. What could she do? She looked around, frantic, her heart pounding. "Won't somebody help me?" she asked.

A neigh filled the air.

Lucky glanced over her shoulder. The stallion was looking at her. He wanted an apple. He wanted attention. But she didn't have time to pet him, to soothe him, to tell him that things would be okay. She needed to warn Pru and Abigail. "I can't talk right now. I have to save Pru and Abigail. Hello? Is anyone here?" she called, hoping someone would magically appear. Someone with a horse!

The stallion neighed again; this time it was high-pitched and anxious. He clearly wanted her attention. He pushed against the gate. Lucky hurried up to the fence. He looked into her eyes, his gaze intense. "You want to get out of there, I know," she said. "But I can't let you go without talking to Mr. Granger. And right now I need to help Pru and Abigail."

The stallion stomped his front hooves. He butted the

gate. Again and again. Mr. Granger had chosen a hefty latch because it didn't budge.

"You're going to hurt yourself," Lucky said, but the stallion wouldn't stop. Tears sprouted, spilling onto Lucky's cheeks. "Please stop; I don't want you to get hurt." She leaned against the fence and hung her head. She didn't know how to help this beautiful mustang. And she didn't know how to help Pru and Abigail. What if her father's project ended up hurting them—or worse? Everything was going wrong. "I don't know what to do."

Something nudged her arm. Warm breath drifted across her face. She looked up. The stallion was gazing at her. Was he trying to tell her something? Lucky couldn't believe what she was thinking. It was crazy. Truly crazy. But maybe…

Maybe it wasn't crazy.

"Do you want to help me?" Lucky asked him. He neighed again.

The only word Lucky could find to describe her feeling at that moment was *instinct*. For there was nothing rational in believing that a wild mustang would offer to help a twelve-year-old girl. And there was nothing rational in believing that a twelve-year-old girl, who'd never even sat on a horse, could ride a wild mustang. But Lucky wasn't thinking with her head at that moment.

With each minute that passed, Pru and Abigail rode closer and closer to Filbert Canyon. No more time could be lost. Lucky unlocked the latch and threw open the gate. She held her breath, expecting the stallion to race to freedom, leaving her in his dust. But he didn't. He waited. Lucky climbed up the fence until she could reach his back. "I don't know how you feel about riding. I don't know how I feel about it, but this is important, so we're just going to figure this out, okay?"

Was it courage that drove her to slide onto his back, or was it the innocent belief that something big was about to happen? Or both?

She was on him—she was sitting on a horse! She looked down. How strange it felt to be that high up. "Okay, we can do this," she said, trying to calm her heart pounding in her ears. With one hand she grabbed hold of his mane. With the other, she pointed in Pru and Abigail's direction. "That way," she said.

And he took off.

"Ahhhh!" Lucky cried, trying to catch her breath. He didn't take long to pick up speed. They passed the schoolhouse and headed toward the open frontier. "Whoa, easy, boy. Maybe this was a bad idea!" Lucky

began to slip to the right, so she clamped with her legs. Then she began to slip to the left, so she clamped harder. She was bouncing around so much, her braid came loose. "P-p-please don't th-th-throw me!" She fell forward, wrapping her arms around his neck. "I'm having second thoughts, in case you're wondering!"

The pace didn't slow, and it felt as if every organ in her body was being pounded and jostled. Trees flew past. She glanced over her shoulder. Miradero was far behind. "Whoa!" she cried as the ground disappeared. The stallion had leaped over a boulder. Her stomach lurched. Was that how it felt to fly? When he landed, she lost her grip. She felt herself sliding forward. Was she going to fly right over his head? As if sensing that she was in danger, he slowed for a moment, long enough for her to find her balance again.

This had been a terrible mistake. Why had she thought she could ride? Her legs were aching. Another leap like that and she'd surely fall off. "Stop," she pleaded. "Stop!" But he didn't obey. What if the stallion wasn't following Pru and Abigail? What if he was heading back to his herd? What if Lucky fell off in the middle of nowhere? She had no canteen of water, no food. And no parasol to shade her from the midday sun. "I'm gonna be in so much trouble!"

Why did people think horseback riding was fun? This was no fun at all! Every time his hooves hit the ground it felt as if *she'd* hit the ground. Her legs were so tense they began to cramp. She couldn't hold on like this much longer.

The image of Lucky's mother standing on horseback filled her mind. How had she managed to find balance with this kind of jarring movement? Then Lucky realized that the horse's galloping wasn't jarring, it was graceful. The problem was that she was fighting against the movement, fighting against the rhythm. She needed to relax. Slowly she sat up, but kept her hands entwined in the stallion's mane. Then she instinctively allowed her aching legs to relax, making them long and pressing her heels down, which instantly felt better. *Breathe*, she told herself. *Calm down and breathe.*

Splash! As the stallion ran across a creek, water sprayed onto Lucky's arms and face. She wiped some droplets off her cheek, then realized—*I'm riding. I'm sitting up and riding.*

Wind blew through the stallion's thick mane and through Lucky's hair. The sun warmed her face, as it warmed his face.

"There they are!" she cried. Pru and Abigail had reached the mountains. They disappeared behind an outcrop. The stallion raced harder. His neck was slick with sweat. How long could he run like this? Lucky had heard about horses being overworked. It happened in the city, occasionally, and it wasn't a pretty sight. He slowed for a sharp turn. And then he came to a standstill, his lungs expanding as he took deep breaths. "Good boy," she told him. Together they'd achieved an amazing, unbelievable feat! She wanted to tell everyone what had just happened. She wanted to send a telegram to Emma. But all that would have to wait. Abigail and Pru were still in danger!

A narrow path stretched before them, with mountains looming on either side. A wooden sign was nailed to a half-rotten post: FILBERT CANYON. There was another sign: DANGER. DO NOT ENTER. DYNAMITE IN USE. But that sign had fallen off the post and was lying on the ground. The girls hadn't seen it.

Lucky looked around. There was no sign of her father or any of the workers. She'd hoped to reach Pru and Abigail before they entered the canyon. Was it safe to follow them? Maybe the railroad work was happening at the other end of the canyon, far, far away. The stallion's ears pricked. And then a familiar voice called, "Hey, Abigail, over here!"

Lucky smiled widely. That was Pru's voice, and it was nearby.

"Can you keep going?" she asked the stallion. He moved forward cautiously, his ears still pricked. Did he sense danger? His breathing was still rapid, but slowing with each step. Fortunately it was cool there, the cliffs shading them from the sun.

BOOM!

Lucky grabbed tightly as the stallion backed up, his head raised, his ears alert. They both looked up at the sky, where a plume of black smoke arose.

The dynamiting had begun.

30

As Abigail sat on the ground, Boomerang nibbled on her hair. She pushed him away. "Boomerang, how many times must I tell you my hair is not food?" she scolded. He didn't seem to care. He was bored because there was nothing to graze on, only cactuses, but luckily he was staying away from those. Pulling spikes out of Boomerang's muzzle was not something Abigail wanted to repeat.

She and Pru had ridden into Filbert Canyon and had stopped near a large boulder that was shaped like a sleeping dog. Walt, one of Mr. Granger's ranch hands, had told Pru that he'd found some beautiful arrowheads at that exact spot. Even though Abigail had heard that Filbert Canyon was off-limits, Pru didn't seem worried. "I hope Walt left a few for us," Pru said as she jabbed the shovel into the dirt.

This canyon was not Abigail's favorite place. It was creepy in there, with steep walls that cast dark shadows, and even steeper ones that cut down to the river. The trails were difficult riding, which Pru loved, but Abigail was the sort who liked to take leisurely rides and enjoy the scenery—not worry about falling off a ledge or rolling down a steep hill. Pru had promised they would stay in the canyon and not touch the side trails, which suited Abigail just fine.

Boomerang pushed against her, wanting more attention. She reached up and scratched his chest. A mournful sound drew their attention. A black vulture circled overhead, searching for carrion. Abigail gulped. "How long are we going to be here?"

Pru dug another clump of dirt and tossed it aside. "It'll take as long as it takes." When Pru set her mind to something, she always saw it through. Abigail knew they wouldn't leave without an arrowhead. "It might go faster if you helped."

"We have only one shovel," Abigail said.

"Yeah, guess that was bad planning on my part. You could sift through the dirt."

"Okay." Abigail was about to pick up one of the dirt clumps when she noticed Chica Linda standing very rigid, her gaze focused on a distant point. A shiver darted up Abigail's spine. She'd grown up on stories about places like this, where cattle rustlers and bandits hid from the law. "What's the matter with Chica Linda? Do you think she hears something?"

Pru looked up and shrugged. "Maybe."

BOOM!

"What was that?" Abigail asked, scrambling to her feet. Boomerang and Chica Linda whinnied with concern.

Pru stopped digging. "I'm not sure. Thunder?"

"Thunder? Seems weird to have thunder today. What if there's lightning, too? We shouldn't be out here if there's lightning."

Pru's eyes narrowed as she looked into the distance. "Who's that?" She pointed as someone on horseback rounded the corner. "Is that…*Lucky*?"

Abigail couldn't believe it. Lucky was charging toward them. And she was sitting, bareback, on the wild stallion. Maybe this was a mirage. The desert could play tricks like this. So Abigail closed her eyes real tight, then opened them. But it was still Lucky and still the wild stallion.

"You've got to get out of here right now!" Lucky shouted to them as the stallion skidded to a stop. Lucky's hair was a wild, windblown mess. Why did she look scared? "They're dynamiting Filbert Canyon!"

"Dynamite?" Pru said, turning to Abigail.

BOOM!

The explosion sounded closer this time. Abigail gasped. Pru dropped her shovel. Boomerang and Chica Linda went nuts, neighing and rearing, their eyes wild as the sound echoed between the canyon walls. A flock of birds took to the sky, followed by black smoke. Abigail grabbed Boomerang's reins, trying to keep him calm. "It's okay, boy. We'll leave right now." She grabbed the saddle horn and pulled herself up.

"Holy moly, that was close," Pru said as she flung herself into her saddle. Reins in hand, she stared at Lucky with disbelief. "When did you learn to—"

BOOM!

There was no time to ask questions. Again the horses reared, but Pru and Abigail held tight. "Okay, that was way too close!" Pru cried. "Let's get outta here!"

Lucky and the stallion took the lead, turning back in the direction they'd come. Abigail and Pru followed. But a rumbling sound filled the air. "Look out!" Pru called, pointing as an avalanche of rocks began rolling down the wall in front of them. The horses skidded to a stop. A cloud of dust filled the air as the rocks landed, blocking the entrance to the canyon.

"Now how do we get out of here?" Lucky asked.

"We have to go this way," Pru said, turning around and leading them to a trail that wound steeply up the canyon wall. "It'll take us up and over." Abigail cringed. She'd been on that trail once before, and it had been a really tricky ride. But what choice did they have? They needed to get out of the canyon as quickly as possible. So she followed as Pru and Chica Linda began riding up the path.

"Wait," Lucky called. Abigail and Pru turned around in their saddles. Lucky and the stallion were at the bottom of the trail. "He doesn't want to go that way," Lucky said. She kicked a few times, but the stallion refused to move forward. He neighed. "He wants to go that way." She pointed in the opposite direction.

"No, this way's better," Pru said. The stallion bolted forward, passing Boomerang and stopping in front of Chica Linda. With eyes blazing, he blocked the path. Lucky held tight to his mane.

"I'm no expert, but I think we should go the other way," Lucky said.

"The other way is longer," Pru told her. "Besides, you don't know these parts."

"It's not me," Lucky said. "It's him."

Abigail trusted Pru, who knew the trails well. But she realized that Lucky was telling the truth. Lucky wasn't making the decision here. She wasn't experienced enough to guide the stallion or make him obey her commands. He was in control, and he'd chosen to block Chica Linda's way. "Pru, maybe we should follow him," Abigail said. "He's a wild horse, so he probably knows all these trails much better than we do."

"I know what I'm doing," Pru said stubbornly. She urged Chica Linda forward. As the palomino tried to step around the stallion, he reared up and slashed at her with his hooves.

"That horse is crazy. Get out of the way!" Pru said angrily.

BOOM!

Another avalanche began to fall, directly up the trail. Before anyone could say another word, the stallion took the lead, with Boomerang and Chica Linda close behind. They raced toward the other path, the one neither Abigail nor Pru had explored. Abigail hadn't turned Boomerang in that direction. He'd chosen to follow. Did he trust the stallion? Maybe they all should.

Abigail gulped when she saw what lay ahead of them. Like the other trail, this one was narrow, but only one side was protected by a rock wall. The other side dropped deep into the canyon, where the river flowed. "I don't like this," Abigail said, her eyes filling with tears. "I don't like this one bit."

"It'll be okay," Pru told her. That was easy for Pru to say because she was one of the best riders in all Miradero. "Just keep focused, and we'll be out of here soon. You ride in the middle." It was odd for Pru to take the last position, but like the horses, she now seemed to trust the stallion's lead.

The stallion slowed his pace, hugging the wall as he stepped along the trail. When he kicked a small rock over the edge, Abigail made the mistake of watching it fall. It was a *very* long drop. She squealed. Boomerang glanced back at her. "Whatever you do, don't look down," she whispered to him. "Just keep going."

She tried to keep her thoughts positive, but she couldn't help imagining the worst. If this trail was blocked by another explosion, they'd have no way to escape. What would they do? Would she ever see her parents again? Would Snips have to go to school without her? How long could she and Boomerang survive on her canteen of water and her blueberry jam sandwich? Abigail didn't want to think about such things. She gripped the reins and turned her focus to Lucky, who didn't have a saddle or reins. One bad move and she could slip right off the stallion's back. "Lucky, are you scared?"

"Yes, definitely."

"Me too."

"Just keep hugging the wall," Pru said. "The horses are too smart to step near the edge."

"Okay," Abigail said, even though no one had ever called Boomerang *smart*. "I think we should talk about something to keep our minds busy. Otherwise I might get too scared to keep going!" Boomerang snorted. Then he bumped into the stallion's rump. The stallion turned his head and gave Boomerang a warning glance.

"Okay, I'll start," Lucky said as they rounded a bend in the path. The horses loosened more rocks, which rolled off the edge and down into the abyss. "This reminds me of a book I just finished. It's called *Journey to the Center of the Earth*. Have you read it?"

"No," they both replied.

"Well, there's this professor and he has a secret map that supposedly leads to the center of the earth. So he takes his nephew and a guide, and they go into a volcano."

"On purpose?" Pru asked.

"Yep." Lucky paused as they turned another corner.

"Keep talking," Abigail pleaded as more rocks fell.

"Well, they descend into the volcano, all the way down, where they find this giant cavern at the center of the earth, with a beach and an ocean." Lucky went on to describe the world she'd read about, and Abigail was very happy to have someone who liked to talk as much as she did. It made her feel less frightened. Boomerang seemed more relaxed, too; his ears turned toward Lucky. "And there's all this other weird stuff down there, like giant mushrooms and giant bugs."

"Ick," Abigail said. "My brother loves bugs."

"How do they get out of the cavern?" Pru asked.

"Well, they build a raft so they can travel on the ocean. And their raft gets sucked into this other volcano, and they get blasted to the surface!"

Another explosion thundered in the distance, followed by the sound of more falling rocks. Abigail squealed again, but this time it was with glee, for they'd turned another corner, and a new sight awaited them. "We're out!" she cried. "We made it!"

Relieved to be out in the open, the horses broke into a gallop, getting some distance from the rock walls. Then they came to a stop and turned. Black smoke rose above the canyon.

Lucky slid off the stallion's back. "Looks like I owe you another apple," she told him. Abigail couldn't believe it. He wasn't acting wild at all. He was even letting Lucky hug him.

Pru and Abigail both dismounted. "You saved our lives," Pru said to Lucky.

Lucky shrugged. "It wasn't me. It was...well, he doesn't have a name, but he was the one who saved you."

"I still don't understand," Pru said. "I thought you couldn't ride. How did you—"

"Are you out of your minds?" The loud voice was unmistakable. Mr. Granger rode toward them, with Lucky's dad and some ranch hands riding at his side. Mr. Prescott dismounted and pulled Lucky into a hug. Mr. Granger jumped to the ground and grabbed Pru. At first he hugged her, but then he held her at arm's length. "Pru, I can't believe you did that. You girls could have been killed." His face was nearly as red as his bandana.

"Dad, we're okay," Pru said apologetically. "I'm really sorry I worried you."

Abigail was glad her parents weren't there. She'd gotten into trouble yesterday after picking all the lettuce in the garden for Boomerang. If her parents knew she'd been riding her horse in an off-limits area, they'd forbid her from riding. She'd lose Boomerang and be stuck with Señor Carrots.

"Didn't you see the danger signs?" Mr. Prescott asked his daughter.

"No," Pru said.

"When we saw you riding out of the canyon, you scared the daylights out of us!" Mr. Granger said, more worried than angry. "It's going to be a long time before I let you on a horse again!" He grabbed a rope from his saddle and looped it over the stallion's neck. Abigail watched with amazement. The stallion didn't try to escape. He didn't buck or rear. He just stood next to Lucky.

Pru stuck her hands in her pocket and looked down at her feet. "I'm sorry, Dad, it's just…"

"It's my fault, sir." Lucky stepped forward. She pushed her tangled hair from her eyes and looked up at Mr. Granger. What was she doing? None of this had been her fault. She'd saved them. Abigail and Pru looked at each other with confusion. "You see, I was taking this horse for a ride, but since I don't actually know how to ride, Pru and Abigail saved me. I got stuck in the canyon, and they showed me the way out. I'm so sorry."

"Lucky, whose horse is that?" Mr. Prescott asked.

"It's my horse," Mr. Granger said with puzzlement.

Mr. Prescott frowned as he addressed his daughter. "Is this true?"

"Yes, I took him out of Mr. Granger's corral," Lucky admitted. "I wanted to ride him. He's the horse I saw from the train. The one the *mesteñeros* caught."

"This is very serious," Mr. Prescott said. "You can't take someone else's horse."

Abigail began to squirm. This wasn't fair. Lucky

shouldn't be in trouble. "Wait…" she said, but Pru stepped forward.

"Dad, you've got it all wrong," Pru said. "I'm the one who wanted to look for arrowheads. Abigail said Filbert Canyon was off-limits, but I didn't think it would be dangerous. I got stubborn and didn't listen. Lucky saw us heading out here and she rode the stallion to warn us. She ended up saving us because the stallion led us down a different path, one I didn't know about. That's how we got out."

Everyone looked at Mr. Granger, waiting for his reaction. Abigail was used to Pru's father. He was strict and he had a hot temper, but he was also a genuinely nice man. He and Pru often quibbled about stuff but in the end, they always loved each other.

Mr. Granger scratched his black beard, moving his gaze between Pru and Lucky. "Two different stories," he said. "Which one is true?"

This time, Abigail stepped forward. "Pru's telling the truth. Lucky and the stallion saved us."

Now everyone was looking at Lucky and the wild mustang. He rested his chin on her right shoulder while she scratched his cheek. They sure seemed close. *How is that possible?* Abigail wondered. Lucky didn't ride horses, and according to Maricela, she didn't even like them!

Mr. Granger pushed his cowboy hat up his forehead and glared at the mustang. "No one should be able to ride that horse. I haven't broken him yet."

"He's not broken?" Mr. Prescott smiled with surprise. "Well, I guess Lucky's a natural."

Mr. Granger looked from Lucky to the stallion and cleared his throat. He turned toward Lucky. "Young lady," he said, "seeing that you and the stallion saved Abigail and my daughter today..." He held out the rope. "You just became the owner of one hardheaded horse."

"What?" Lucky stopped scratching and her arm fell to her side. "He's...mine?"

"Al, are you sure?" Mr. Prescott asked.

"He saved my girl's life. I couldn't be more sure about anything." He pressed the rope into Lucky's hand, and she took it. "Heck, he won't let anyone else get near him. That horse has got a heck of a lot of spirit."

Lucky gasped. "That's perfect. His name is...Spirit."

Abigail clapped her hands in delight. "This is the best day ever! Lucky, now you can go riding with us." Lucky pressed her forehead against the stallion's. Abigail smiled. Yes, they really did belong together. What a perfect match.

Lucky turned to Mr. Granger. "Thank you, sir, but are you sure about this?"

"As sure as a pig in a puddle," Mr. Granger said with a smile. "He's yours."

"Thank you for giving Spirit to me, but…" Lucky took a deep breath. This was the right thing to do. "Spirit can't be owned. When I was riding him, I felt…free. And if it's all right with you, that's how I'd like him to stay." She slipped the rope from his neck. "Free." She kissed his cheek. And then she stepped away.

As if he somehow understood what had just happened, Spirit turned and raced away toward the distant hills.

"Good-bye," Lucky said, wiping a tear from her eye. Abigail put her arm around Lucky's shoulder. Pru joined them, as did Boomerang and Chica Linda, watching as the stallion beat his wild rhythm across the frontier.

And then, Spirit was gone.

31

Immediately following the incident with the girls,
Lucky's dad ordered the workers to place more DANGER
signs around Filbert Canyon. Then he told them to take
the rest of the day off; they would start again in the
morning. When he and Lucky got home, he explained
to Cora what had happened. "I'm never taking my eyes
off you," Cora declared, hugging Lucky until she turned
blue. "Stealing a wild horse and nearly getting blown
up!" Cora placed her hand on the wall, steadying herself.
Was she going to faint for the first time in her life? The
incident strengthened her resolve to leave Miradero as
soon as possible. "Don't cry, sweetheart," Cora said,
wiping a tear from Lucky's cheek. "We'll see your father
as often as possible. I promise." Cora mistook the tears
for sadness, when really they were brought on by joy.
Lucky had accomplished her task—to set the stallion free.
It was the best feeling in the world.

"Aunt Cora, about leaving," she said. "I've been
thinking, and—"

"Hey, what's that sound?" Jim interrupted as voices
rose outside.

Lucky, Cora, and Jim stepped onto the porch.

Dozens of people were walking toward the house. Lucky recognized some from town, others from school.

"Oh dear, I'm not dressed for company." Cora grabbed her pheasant-feather hat and plunked it onto her head.

"Hello," Jim called as they neared. "What's going on here?"

The people gathered at the base of the steps. Everyone was carrying something to eat. There were cakes and pies, bowls of potato salad and sandwiches. Snips had two handfuls of carrots. The mayor and his wife were there as well. Even Maricela held a plate of cookies, though she was the only person not smiling. "We've come to thank Lucky for all she did today," Mr. Granger said. "And to officially welcome the Prescotts to Miradero, their new home."

"Well, that's mighty nice of you," Jim said. He gave Lucky and Cora a long, thoughtful look, for only the three of them knew the truth—that Cora and Lucky might be leaving.

"So, you gonna make us stand here all day?" Mr. Granger asked with a chuckle. Then he held up a platter. "Wouldn't you rather eat my famous barbecued ribs?"

Lucky's stomach growled. Those ribs looked amazing. She jabbed her dad with her elbow. "Uh, yes, of course," Jim said. "Let's eat!"

Cora stood quietly to the side, watching as the kitchen table was brought out from the house, along with chairs and benches. Some blankets were set on the ground. People ate the ribs with their hands instead of using a fork and knife. A few of the men used their shirtsleeves as napkins. Cora's expression was so twitchy, Lucky thought her face might crack like porcelain. How could Lucky break the news that she'd decided to stay? She didn't want her aunt to feel obligated to remain in Miradero, just because she was staying. She wanted her aunt to be happy. And she wasn't happy here. Poor Cora.

"Hello." A woman walked up to Cora and extended her hand. "I'm Althea. I run the Tanglefoot Inn." Cora looked puzzled at first, for ladies of society didn't normally shake hands. But she took Althea's. "I saw your posters. How was your meeting?"

Cora sighed. "No one came to my meeting. Apparently no one in this town is interested in my causes. I have no place here."

"No place here?" Althea put her hands on her broad hips. "No one came to your meeting because no one knew what it was. What in the world is a Ladies' Social Betterment Society?"

Cora's hand flitted to her collar. "Why, it's a group where we have discussions about important matters, and we raise money to bring art and culture to the community and to help those in need."

"Why didn't you say so in the first place?" Althea said with a laugh. "We've got one of those already. It's the Ladies' Aid Society. I'm the president. We meet every Wednesday, and it just so happens we're looking for a treasurer. How about joining us?"

Lucky had never seen her aunt smile so big. "Yes," Cora said breathlessly. "I'd like that very much."

"Come on, I'll introduce you to some of our members." Althea led Cora to one of the tables. Three women scooted down the bench to make room. Althea set a plate of potato salad and ribs in front of Cora and began to tell her about their next fund raiser. Cora absorbed every word, like a thirsty sponge.

As one of Mr. Granger's ranch hands played the banjo, Abigail and Pru sat with Lucky on the porch steps. "You know, we've got plenty of horses at the Ramada," Pru told Lucky. "If you meet us there tomorrow, we'll help you pick one out."

Abigail broke a cookie in two and handed half to Lucky. "Then you can ride with us."

"Really?" It was the thing Lucky had been most craving—the invitation, not the cookie, though she did love oatmeal. "I'll need to check with my dad and aunt, but that sounds great."

As Lucky ate the cookie, she glanced across the yard. Her dad was laughing with Mr. Granger and the mayor. And Cora was chatting with the women from the Miradero Ladies' Aid Society. Cora was so happy, she picked up one of the ribs, *with her fingers*, and took a bite. Lucky wouldn't have believed it if she hadn't seen it with her own eyes.

That tight feeling in Lucky's stomach was gone. She smiled.

She felt as light as air.

That night, as Lucky was climbing into bed, her dad knocked on the door. "Hey, sweet pea," he said. He stood in the doorway, his hands behind his back. "Well, that was an exciting day."

"Yeah, pretty amazing." So much had happened, her head was still spinning. "I told Emma all about it." She pointed to a letter lying on the bedside table.

"You won't be telling Emma in person? Does that mean you're staying?"

"Yes."

"I'm very happy to hear that." He stepped into the room. "You know, when I saw you riding that mustang, for a minute, I thought I saw your mother."

"Really?"

"Yes, really." He kept his hands behind his back. "You not only looked like her, but you rode like her. I'm not sure how to explain it, but you looked…graceful. Like you've been riding all your life."

Lucky sat up very straight. She had something important to say. "Dad…" She took a deep breath. "I think I'm good with horses. They seem to like me. Even Señor Carrots likes me, and he's a donkey. No one else could get Spirit's trust but me. I think it's what I'm good at. I think…I get it from Mom."

"I agree. That's why I want you to have these." He held out a pair of boots.

"Wow!" Lucky scrambled out of bed. "For me?" She couldn't believe this was happening. She knew these boots by heart. She ran her hands over the flames.

"Go ahead, try them on," her dad urged.

She hesitated. This was a huge moment. She'd learned so much about herself in such a short time—that she could ride, that horses trusted her—things that she and her mother had in common. But stepping into her mother's boots felt even scarier than climbing onto the stallion's back. What if they didn't fit? What if she could never *really* fill her mother's shoes?

Lucky slipped her feet inside and they fit perfectly.

She walked around the room, getting a feel for the high arch and the curve of the toe. The boots were well worn, and that made them extra comfortable. "Thank you, Dad."

"You're very welcome."

Lucky took these boots as a really good sign. Now was the time to broach the subject. "Dad, Pru said that if I go to the Ramada tomorrow, she and Abigail will help me pick out a horse. I want to learn to ride." She waited, worried that he'd say no for all the same reasons Cora always said no. "Will you let me learn? Will you let me take lessons? Please?"

"As long as you promise to stay out of areas that are being dynamited," he said with a furrowed brow.

"I promise!"

"Then riding lessons sound good to me."

That night, the dream came again, but this time it wasn't Cowgirl Betty who stood on the stage. Milagro Navarro, in her circus dress and red-and-brown boots, held out her hand to her daughter. "What am I doing here?" Lucky asked.

"You're gonna show them what you're made of," her

mother replied. When Lucky looked into the audience, she recognized so many upturned faces—Pru and Abigail, Miss Flores and Snips, Turo and Mr. Granger, her father and her grandpa, Mr. and Mrs. MacFinn, Emma and Aunt Cora. Even Maricela was there.

Shadow nudged Lucky with his muzzle, urging her to climb into the saddle. Milagro smiled at Lucky and handed her the reins. This time there was no hesitation. Lucky grabbed the saddle horn, stepped into the stirrup, and swung her leg like a professional. Shadow shifted as Lucky settled in, preparing for her command. Then, reins in hand, she faced the ring of fire.

And together, they jumped through.

32

Spirit was happy to be reunited with his herd, but it wasn't the same. While he belonged with them, something was missing—something that hadn't been missing before. And that is why he went back.

He stood on the hill, his head held high, watching and waiting.

Below the hill, in the corral, the men with ropes saw him, but they didn't chase him. They left him alone and turned their attention to the other horses, the ones they'd tamed. They knew he wasn't meant for them.

But where was she?

His ears pricked at the sound of nearby footsteps. Three girls walked toward the barn—the girl with the yellow mane, the girl with the black mane, and the girl who knew his name.

He neighed. She turned, saw him, and began running up the hill, her long mane flowing behind her.

"Spirit!" she cried, holding out her arms. She pressed her face into his neck. "You came back."

Yes, he'd come back. Despite the joyous reunion with his family, he realized that he now belonged in two worlds—the world of his herd and the world of this girl.

She had set him free and he would never forget. For a horse will always remember kindness.

He dipped his head, then bowed his front legs so she could climb onto his back.

"Lucky?" the smaller girl called. "Aren't you going to pick out a horse?"

"I don't have to," his girl called back. "He picked me!"

He waited for her friends to join them, with the horses he now trusted—the one with the white spots and the one with the golden coat. He waited for his girl to find her balance, to secure her hands in his mane. "Let's go, Spirit!" she cried.

"Let's go, Boomerang!"

"Let's go, Chica Linda!"

The morning sun warmed the prairie as hearts and hooves beat a wild rhythm.

Author's Note

Dear Reader,

While I hope you enjoyed this story, I want to point out that this is not a piece of historical fiction. While some of it is historically accurate, this is not meant to represent the true American West or the Victorian age. It is pure fiction, set in a fictitious location in the American West, in a time in the nineteenth century, and that is all. Please enjoy it as fiction.

I have been extremely blessed in my writing career because some really amazing projects have come my way. When Kara Sargent, my lovely editor at Little, Brown, asked if I'd be interested in writing a novel for DreamWorks Animation, I nearly fainted. Do you even have to ask? Yes! And when she told me that the story would be based on *Spirit: Stallion of the Cimarron*, I was thrilled. That had been one of my daughter's favorite movies. We'd watched it together countless times. I even knew all the songs by heart. So I flew down to the DreamWorks Animation campus in Glendale, California, met with a whole bunch of really nice people, and the journey began.

I would like to begin by thanking Aury Wallington, the DreamWorks writer at the helm of this new Spirit series. Her script was the inspiration for my novel and served as the novel's framework. Thank you, Aury, for providing me with such a fun world in which to play. There are many more people involved in this project, and I'm very grateful for their help. Thanks to Rich Burns, Laura Sreebny, Katherine Nolfi, Robert Taylor, Lauren Bradley, Megan Startz, Harriet Murphy, Corinne Combs, Barb Layman, Mike Sund, David Wiebe, Rebecca Goldberg, Tiffany Howell, Jackie Chan, and Natalie Wei.

At Little, Brown Publishing, working alongside Kara Sargent, I'd like to thank Mara Lander, Christina Quintero, Kristina Pisciotta, Lindsay Walter-Greaney, Dani Valladares, Dan Letchworth, Allegra Green, Carol Scatorchio, and Victoria Stapleton.

Big thanks to my dear friend, Jeremy Bishop, for patiently answering all my train questions. And thanks also to Megan Chance, Sue and Faith Kerrigan, and Vicky Poole for answering all my horse questions. While I still did most of my writing at Hot Shots Java in Poulsbo, where LeAnne Musgrove, AJ Stokes and their staff keep me caffeinated, I added a new coffeehouse to my routine—Cups—owned by the lovely Wanda Winker.

Without these welcoming baristas, I'd be stuck in my office writing, and that's no fun at all.

And, as always, thanks to my agent, Michael Bourret, for making the business side of writing easy peasy. And to my family, Bob, Walker, and Isabelle, who keep my spirit riding free.

Happy reading, everyone!